After All This Time, Still

OLIVE ROSE STEELE

This book is a work of fiction. Some names of actual places have been included. However, similarities to real persons or events are entirely coincidental. All depictions are the product of the author's imagination.
Copyright © 2021 Olive Rose Steele
All rights reserved.
ISBN: 9798651863105

After all this time, Still: A Novel /
Olive Rose Steele

For information contact:
www.blackwoodself-publishingmadeeasy.com

First Edition: November 2021.
Printed in Canada.

PROLOGUE ONE

But if you love and must needs have desires, let these be your desires:
To melt and be like a running brook that sings its melody to the night.
To know the pain of too much tenderness.
To be wounded by your own understanding of love;
And to bleed willingly and joyfully.
—Kahlil Gibran, The Prophet

Sunday afternoon, June 7, 2009, sunny, the temperature right, bright blue sky with fluffy, white, drifting clouds—a glorious summer's day; the blooms red and yellow, the grass lay green on the ground from overnight rain, people moving about.

On that beautiful day, when Sheldon Jason Morgan stood in the Rotunda of Tower Two, the Emerald Towers, next to his wife, Blossom Mae Black, he could not have known it would be the last time he would be with her. Sandy, the papergirl circled the

AFTER ALL THIS TIME, Still

Rotunda a few times; her ponytail lifted as she pumped the pedals. Each time she passed by where Blossom had been sitting; she smiled, her tiny hands gripping the Bar of her bike.

Mrs. Cicci returned from the nearby bakery; Mr. Cicci lagged with Mr. Gould, his walking partner. Finally, Mrs. Cicci entered the turn at the Rotunda, brown paper bag in hand, the end part of her freshly baked bread showing. "Hello, Mr. and Mrs. Morgan; nice day today," she said in her cheery voice and entered an open elevator. Blossom and Sheldon flashed pleasant smiles.

Sam, the security guard, stepped out of his booth. "Good day, Mr. and Mrs. Morgan," he said with a smile. He was ready to start a conversation; Sheldon enveloped Blossom's shoulders; Sam turned and walked back into his booth.

Nothing about the day seemed out of order, except when the small bus with the writing *Ethica Mature Lifestyles* pulled up in front of Tower Two lobby. On other Sundays, Sheldon would pack a picnic basket in the trunk of Blossom's wheelchair-accessible van and be off for a day at the Park. However, the Sunday afternoon in question was out of order in ways Sheldon would never forget.

Sheldon recognized the small bus transporting Blossom to *Ethica Mature Lifestyles*, where she would rest and mend after a stroke. He will miss her. His heart quaked and shattered into tiny pieces; he wanted to hand her a piece of his heart.

Earlier in the morning, Sheldon and Blossom ate breakfast at their favorite Café. The Sunday group were all familiar faces—neighbors, church people, writers, students—some sitting upright around tables, others lay back in cushioned chairs, all enjoying a hot drink. Blossom had coffee and a tea biscuit with a teaspoon of jelly on the side; Sheldon had coffee and a toasted bagel with crème cheese; neither wanted a big breakfast. Sheldon had been thinking about his quick return to *Ethica Mature Lifestyles* to carry Blossom back home to Montego Bay.

"Mrs. Johnson will come once a week to dust our Suite and keep it tidy so that when you are there, everything will be the same as when we left." So Blossom said once Sheldon settled her comfortably at the table. Sheldon mumbled, "uh-huh."

"Sam will be extra diligent, I am sure, knowing neither you nor I will be occupying our suite for a while." Sheldon bit into his bagel and took a mouthful of his coffee with a sulk on his face.

"Don't be sad, sweetheart; I am only going away for a brief time; I will recover quickly. Dr. Steiner, Dr. Lee, and I are confident the degenerative disorder that crept in will calm down." Sheldon smiled, "I, too, am confident still I will miss you."

While Sheldon waited with Blossom in the Rotunda, his thoughts veered to when he and Blossom spent hours picnicking in Marie Curtis Park. The crusty age-old trees with the scars they carry from sawed-off branches came to mind; he wondered if they were still standing.

The small bus from *Ethica Mature Lifestyles* waited. Sheldon looked sideways at Blossom; "Shall we go, honey?" he said softly. Blossom looked up into his eyes. He held her gaze for an extended moment.

Sheldon slowly knelt by her side. He pressed both her knuckles against his chest and brushed a kiss on her lips. He knew he would be miserable without Blossom.

Blossom inhaled deeply.

The lift raised her wheelchair gently onto the bus.

The attendant settled her securely.

Sheldon stood on the curb—waving.

"I love you," Sheldon mimed.

"I love you too," Blossom mimed back.

The small bus moved out gently onto the freeway en route to a new place and beginning. They were deeply in love, and the moment suggested they would be together soon.

Suddenly, doubt crept in to dampen Sheldon's spirit. It would be unkind if fate took Blossom away and left him lifeless.

The following day, Sheldon boarded a plane bound for Montego Bay. In a letter to Blossom, he wrote—

Montego Bay,
June 2009
My darling Bloss,
I am counting the days until I see you.
It will not be long before I return for you;
I will have you in my arms, where you belong.
I love you so much. Your husband,
Sheldon.

PROLOGUE TWO

When you love you should not say, "God is in my heart," but rather, "I am in the heart of God."
And think not you can direct the course of love, for love, if it finds you, worthy, directs your course
—*Kahlil Gibran,* The Prophet

Ethica Mature Lifestyles, August 2010

After a peaceful hour of solitude, Blossom exhaled what turned out to be her last breath and closed her eyes. "Good afternoon, Mrs. Morgan."

Moira had come with Blossom's afternoon tea. She seemed to have been napping in her cushioned adjustable chair.

Moira touched Blossom lightly on her shoulder; she tilted to one side. Then, Moira touched her again, and Blossom dropped to the floor.

Moira called out, "Call 911, someone—please. Mrs. Morgan is in distress."

Blossom had been sitting by the window watching daylight turn softer, which was when Moira came with late afternoon tea; everything remained the same at *Ethica Mature Lifestyles*. Deviations were dreary days with draperies drawn, chilly nights without Sheldon's warm body alongside her, visits from Dr. Lee, her physician, and Gordon Rusk, her trusted lawyer.

The stretch from her window on the eighth floor is vast. On a clear day, she could see many miles of Lake Ontario glistening in the magnificent sun and white streaks from passing planes crisscrossing the blue skies. Blossom looked away from the window; for a long moment, she studied her arms and fingers; then, she looked at the withered tree trunks and became frightened.

"I am like the dry bramble I see in the yard outside my window; I can't keep this together much longer, honey." So she had told Sheldon over the phone.

"You will be well, my love, for my sake." Sheldon had said. Still, Blossom sensed she was in her final days even as she waited at *Ethica Mature Lifestyles* for Sheldon to come; she remembered the lines he wrote in a letter.

My darling Bloss, you make me smile whenever I think about you. You, my sweetheart, have taught me the true meaning of love, and even as I am yearning for you and counting the days until I have you in my arms, the truth is I merely exist with you being so far away. I love you, Sheldon.

Blossom Mae Black, 62 years old, wealthy beyond her memory. Her eyes show the hint of green she inherited from her mother's side of the family; her skin still invites a touch. Her shoulder-length hair, usually laid across her back, was now set in a bun at her nape. Jacques, her hairdresser, had suggested a bob cut when he had washed her hair. She touched her bony cheeks and quickly pulled her fingers back, afraid to acknowledge her fading beauty.

Blossom was the beloved daughter of Whitfield Black, the famous leader of a Reggae band, and Margarita Black. They had hoped their daughter would be a ballet dancer like Margarita. But, instead, Blossom's ambitions took her far afield in a foreign country, much to her parents' disappointment.

Her mother had been the person who gave unconditional love; her father saw her as his little girl, to be protected, always and forever. She wondered if she had done enough to show gratitude to her parents; because she was their only offspring.

She recalls a plan to holiday with Sheldon in Istanbul. She had always been fascinated by the architecture, churches with high ceilings, Museums, pristine beaches, and exotic foods that she had seen in holiday catalogs—Istanbul, Constantinople—no different.

"Why do you say Constantinople, Mom?" She had asked her mother when she was a little girl. "Istanbul was Constantinople, dear," her mother had answered and then went on to tell her the history of how Constantinople became Istanbul. She always thought her mother had visited Istanbul to have known so much about the place. Only her mother's grandparents were from Turkey, and they had told her mother tales and history. All the same, Istanbul was a destination she still desired to see.

She let out a soft sigh; and turned her head toward the open door. She thought she saw a silhouette of someone standing in the hallway.

Blossom's thoughts moved along slowly.

Giving birth to the child of Sheldon Morgan was what she had planned. It is true the consequences of her plan to bear Sheldon's child would ruin lives and cause untold heartaches, but Blossom had been resolute; she would only be content with an outward sign of her love for him.

Perhaps there's a price I must pay for such an ill-conceived plan; fate has chased me down, got into my face, and made me regret—this is the price I paid for loving you
—Cry Tough.

Despite her mistakes and poor choices, Blossom was endearing at the same time. Her son, Jason Sheldon Black, had said goodbye when he was three months old, an accident she would never forget. Jason left her with a scar on her heart and a permanent disability. It had been fifteen months since she lived at *Ethica Mature Lifestyles*, and she counted the days till she would be released, though the days appeared to merge and became long and dreary.

PART ONE

For even as love crowns you, so shall he crucify you.
Even as he is for your growth so is he for your pruning.
Even as he ascends to your height and caress your tenderest branches that quiver in the sun,
So shall he descend to your roots and shake them in their clinging to the earth.
Like sheaves of corn he gathers you unto himself
He threshes you to make you naked,
He sifts you to free you from your husks.
He grinds you to whiteness.
He kneads you until you are pliant;
And then he assigns you to his secret fire, that you may become sacred bread for God's holy feast.
—*Kahlil Gibran,* The Prophet.

CHAPTER ONE

September 30, 2010, Toronto, Canada

Sheldon Morgan arrived at Pearson Airport in Toronto on a calm day in September with worry on his mind. He was glad to be back where people were polite, and Evian bottled water was plentiful. He had been through the airport several times, but this time he had mixed feelings when he stepped out to the pickup curb and hailed a taxi.

"The Emerald Towers in Etobicoke," he said to the driver.

His wife Blossom had been ill for many months at *Ethica Mature Lifestyles*, and her deteriorating health alarmed him. Unfortunately, the breakthrough medicine, believed to be the cure for Blossom's illness, had not been successful.

The prospect of seeing Blossom in her

reported declining state hung over his head like a dark, heavy rain cloud waiting to explode. When he reached his home at Building Two, Emerald Towers, he was emotionally exhausted from conflicting thoughts in his head. He kicked off his loafers in the vestibule of his Suite and turned on the lights.

Rested on the ledge atop the fireplace where his son Jason's photograph used to be, was a fresh bunch of flowers in an antique tray. He read the note attached. *Welcome home, my love—Bloss.*

Sheldon was glad to be home. He wandered around his familiar Suite, where he had spent beautiful years with Blossom. Blossom's butter-soft recliner, placed by the side of his equally soft armchair, remained in the original spot in front of the Bay window overlooking 403 highway. Unfortunately, the orchids that Blossom loved so much were no longer on the window ledge. The main bedroom is still beautifully decorated. His eyes caught the large portrait of Blossom on the wall across from the mirrored entrance. He smiled at having Blossom back in luxurious Suite 2108 and his arms.

Blossom's absence from the Suite troubled him much, and he did not want to be there without her. He had secretly considered making Suite 2108 available for rental since it had been mostly unoccupied. He wanted to keep it locked up, yet he wanted someone to occupy it; finally, he chose to auction some contents, except for Blossom's prized pieces, and kept the Suite locked up. "We'll live here, in Montego Bay … you love the terrific weather ... it does your body good," Sheldon had said to Blossom in one of his regular phone conversations.

"I don't know, Sheldon; this time, the situation is more overwhelming. It is becoming too much for me to endure." However, it was evident from the sound of her voice that she, too, was aware of her longevity. So, this time, he hoped she would be well enough to return with him to Montego Bay.

He was famished. The intercom in his Suite announced his take-out fish and chips had arrived. He telephoned Blossom at *Ethica Mature Lifestyles*.

"Hello, Sweetheart," he said, hearing his wife's voice, "The plane landed at Pearson this afternoon at 2.30—how have you been keeping, honey?"

"Wonderful"

"The bouquet you sent me is beautiful, Bloss; thank you."

"Miss you, hon; I am anxious to leave this place—it's making me crazy." Blossom sounded exhausted.

"Hang in there, baby; I'm coming for you."

Since Sheldon went away, all Blossom asked of him was to come back for her; she would rather be in her home, surrounded by her favorite things, than be at *Ethica Mature Lifestyles*. Blossom Black, a wealthy woman beyond her comprehension, could purchase the necessary health services and assistance she needed to live everyday life. Twenty-four/seven therapeutics were essential and made available wherever she found herself. Her medical team recommended *Ethica Mature Lifestyles* as the place to be during recovery, with Sheldon domiciled in Jamaica.

"I will come for you the day after tomorrow, honey—I scope out spare parts for equipment at Caterpillar tomorrow morning, and my appointment with Gordon is in the afternoon."

"See you soon, my love; see you soon."

Blossom's stay at *Ethica Mature Lifestyles*, the best place in convalescence living, was to have been short-term care as she recovered from the stroke that occurred after the death of her son Jason at three months. But unfortunately, a degenerative disease was diagnosed later, worsening her health. Her physician, Dr. Lee, had been treating the ailment, and though he predicted it might slow down her recovery from the stroke, he believed Blossom would be well enough to return to her own home.

In considering Blossom's ill health, Sheldon tried to decide what to do with his earthmoving and construction business in Jamaica. Blossom had suggested he made his mind up and sold it—a suggestion he had been reluctant to consider.

"It has to be this way a while longer, honey—the right buyer hasn't come along yet," he had said when Blossom pressed for a resolution. Between slow sips of green tea, he telephoned the front desk.

"Sam—Mr. Morgan here, tell my chauffeur, Mason, to be in the Rotunda tomorrow morning at eight sharp."

"Yes, Sir."

As Sheldon was exiting Suite 2108 the following morning, the phone rang.

"Top of the morning, Sir"—it was Michael Dixon, his Project Manager calling from Montego Bay.

"Mister Doug threatens to cause trouble at the West Hill site again. Sir—the situation could turn ugly." So continued Dixon.

Doug Williams, the Head of his family's construction company, was a thorn in Sheldon's side; they never got along; instead, they butted heads often and took each other before the Magistrate.

The two were fierce competitors and regular bidders for earthmoving and construction contracts from aluminum ore companies in Jamaica's bauxite industry.

Sheldon once punched out Doug Williams's false teeth in a fight when Doug laughed in his face and said, in his drunken drawl, "I hear your *people* in Toronto is sharing her bed with another man," referring to Blossom. "Shut your big mouth, or I'll break your jawbone—you three-inch prick," Sheldon shouted in Doug's face as blood spewed out from his mouth.

"You know I am telling the truth. You were too busy stealing old-man Fairweather's business right from under his nose—asshole."

It was no secret; Sheldon had taken over and run George Fairweather's business since the older man became frail. "It was never my intention to run the place like a two-bit tool shed," Sheldon had said. But, to the dismay of the Williams Brothers, Sheldon turned Fairweather's small establishment into a million-dollar enterprise that became the main point of conversation in Jamaica's earth-moving industry.

Suddenly the fire alarm in Building Two began to squeal; Sheldon pressed the telephone receiver hard against his ears to hear through the loud, high-pitched noise; he started down the exit stairs; other residents joined as everyone made the downward trek.

"Dixon," Sheldon said, still holding the phoned to his ears, "I will be back in Montego Bay in a few days; continue until I come …."

"Okay, Boss, I'll take care of things."

Sheldon stopped short of saying aloud; *Dixon, it's your damn job to run the place, do your job.*

The gust of cool air that greeted him when he pushed open the exit door was refreshing. Residents stood in groups at designated areas, and a fire truck was in place. Sheldon's Brier Blue, Chevrolet Corvette, usually stored in the underground garage, was parked in Tower Two Rotunda, engine running, and Mason holding the open passenger-side door. Sheldon slid into the seat and buckled his seatbelt.

"Do you know if there is a fire?"

"Not a real fire, Mr. Morgan; a fire drill." Sheldon sighed in relief.

"First, I will go to the Caterpillar showroom on Lakeshore Road and then downtown Toronto."

"Sure, Mr. Morgan."

The highway drive was slow. Sheldon's eyes roamed from his car to the cars driving close by.

"What are you thinking, Mr. Morgan?"

"Should've taken the train," Sheldon answered. Morning traffic along the QEW highway ground to a standstill.

"Road repairs on the Express Way account for the bottleneck, Mr. Morgan."

Sheldon adjusted his seatbelt. "Please turn the heat down, Mason; the car is too hot."

"Sorry, Sir." Mason glanced sideways at Sheldon.

"Sir, we will be on time for your appointment."

"It's all the same, Mason," Sheldon said, still wrapped up in deep thought.

"Your spare parts will be packed and shipped to Montego Bay in a week, Mr. Morgan." So said the seller who served Sheldon at Caterpillar.

The ramp to get back on the freeway had backed up; it was clear the journey into Toronto would be a slow one. The bumper-to-bumper crawl into the city ended at the city line below Front Street. Vehicles slowed considerably at Bay and Front Streets to allow commuters to cross safely from the train station. Pedestrians fanned out in all directions and dodged in and out of office buildings, holding coffee mugs. Downtown Toronto was a hub of activities, especially during morning rush hour and afternoon lunchtime

Peggy had briefed Sheldon on crucial topics for

discussion with his Toronto attorney, Gordon Rusk—among them, Gordon's responsibilities and efficient management of the legal elements of Sheldon's expanding family businesses at the Canadian end. And, with Blossom's inability to clearly express her desires, Sheldon insists on Gordon's loyalty.

Finally, Mason stopped at the curb where Gordon Rusk had been standing outside the lobby door of his office building. He had been waiting to receive Sheldon. When Gordon saw Sheldon approaching, Gordon smiled.

"Good morning, Mr. Morgan—how was your commute into the city?" he asked, a subtle hint that he had observed the traffic situation. Sheldon extended his right hand for a handshake.

"Traffic was slow but steady—glad we made it on time," Sheldon answered. Both men entered an ascending elevator to the 35th floor.

"Each time I come to see you, the elevators take me higher," Sheldon remarked.

"Glad you are enjoying the ride," Gordon said with an amount of prudence.

"Are we in the CN Tower?" Sheldon asked as he exited the elevators.

"This is the Scotia Plaza Tower," Gordon grinned, delighted that Sheldon noticed the setting.

Born and bred in Toronto, Gordon Rusk loves the city, and therefore he would get a bit touchy when out-of-towners portrayed tall downtown Toronto structures as the CN Tower. But, of course, there are other tall buildings downtown, he would tell confused visitors. Still, if the CN tower reminded people of Toronto, so be it.

Gordon Rusk and Sheldon Morgan entered his law office through double glass front doors that parted on approach, walked past the reception area, and turned to his private office. Imported Mahogany wood furniture, fine paintings, and expensive carpeting welcome Sheldon into this principled lawyer's office.

Gordon pointed Sheldon to a cushioned wing chair. "Your green tea will be here in a moment," Gordon said and pressed a gold button on his desk.

Sheldon wasted no time; he dived into the task at hand and said, "Gordon, I pay you well for the legal work you do for my family…." he trailed off. Sheldon pushed back his chair, stretched out his long legs, and crossed them at the ankle while observing Gordon as he moved papers around on his desk like playing cards.

Gordon shuffled in his big chair. It gave a soft squeak. He leaned over, lowered his eyes to the plain white paper in front of him, and pulled a pen from its holder. He scribbled.

In his Last Will, David Austin Clark, the former husband of Blossom, bequeathed a substantial legacy to his disabled son, who was already living in a home for people with disabilities. But, sadly, the boy's mother was only interested in the size of the boy's inheritance.

"I will convince the boy's witch of a mother to allow me to get him to live in Ontario so I can direct his care," Blossom had confided in Gordon Rusk.

Gordon looked up and met Sheldon's eyes. "I hope I've served you well all these years, Mr. Morgan."

Sheldon put an index finger to his lips, pressing back his reply.

Gordon Rusk had been a lawyer to Blossom before Sheldon became Blossom's husband. So Gordon knew a lot about the family history. Moreover, Sheldon trusted that Gordon would be loyal to him just as he had been loyal to David Clark, the deceased husband of Blossom. So when Blossom appointed Gordon Rusk to be the Power of Attorney for her general affairs, Sheldon felt confident all would be well.

"I've streamlined the firm to keep up with growth; your family's account will stay with me," Gordon assured Sheldon.

Gordon had always felt ill at ease in the presence of Sheldon Morgan, mainly because he was partial to David Clark. Nevertheless, Gordon was mindful of the financial magnitude of Sheldon Morgan; he hoped he had not misspoken when he told Sheldon about having to hire a new lawyer and separating some accounts.

Sheldon pulled his chair closer to the rim of Gordon's desk and leaned forward. "The Chalet in Collingwood……." he trailed off.

He placed both palms on the edge of Gordon's desk as though he was about to push himself up "….give me a verbal summary of my wife's wealth."

"The entire 21-floor structure, known as Building Two, Emerald Towers; the Winter Chalet in Collingwood; the Summer home in Ocho Rios; ownership of Greenfield Property Development; Marble and Granite Jamaica Limited, cash in your joint bank accounts, stocks, bonds, mutual funds......" he trailed off. Sheldon stood and walked to the large window overlooking the busy street; "My wife would like to see the Chalet in Collingwood renovated and turned into a hotel and convention center. Can you make that happen?"

Gordon leaned back in his big chair, looped his fingers at the back of his head, and said, "I am not sure how I can help you with that, Mr. Morgan."

Sheldon looked over his shoulders at Gordon; he wondered if he had his complete allegiance. He pursed his lips. Sheldon would not readily admit to it, but he was unwilling to accept the slightest hesitancy to any request he made.

"You will find a way to carry out my request—and, Gordon, as my wife's power of attorney for all matters, I have much confidence in how you've managed your assignment so far…keep it that way."

"You are a wise man—how soon do you want me to start on the Chalet renovation, Mr. Morgan?"

"As soon as you hire a builder. My sense is the project might take six months to complete."

"I will start the ball rolling," Gordon said.

"Well," Sheldon said, "I will go down to the Queens Quay and pass away an hour or two listening to the seagulls squawk and watch sailboats on the lake until the rush hour traffic thins out."

Sheldon extended his hand; Gordon shook it, and then Sheldon exited the building. Mason was idling the Corvette at the curb, waiting. Sheldon spotted a nearby restaurant famous for homemade pasta, fresh vegetables, and salads; he sat with Mason and had lunch before going to the Quays.

On returning to Suite 2108, Sheldon dismissed Mason for the night. "Wake me up tomorrow morning at 8, please," he said.

"As you wish, Sir," Mason said.

Sheldon was anxious for a report from Dr. Lee. He hoped there would be a message from him on his phone to say Blossom would be well enough to travel to Montego Bay.

He opened the door of Suite 2108, and immediately the telephone rang.

"Hello, Doc?"

Dr. Lee had always been clear and direct in delivering updates on Blossom's prognosis, though, lately, Sheldon had lost confidence in the advice he had been getting from Dr. Lee.

"Dam it, Lee, I don't have to accept everything you tell me regarding my wife's health."

"I am your wife's physician; Mr. Morgan, I treat your wife based on a diagnosis. You, Sir, believe in what your money can buy, and I respect that; I provide medicine for an illness; I am the one who is working to keep your wife alive. But unfortunately, I must tell you,

Sir, Mrs. Morgan is not well enough to return to Montego Bay." Both men were annoyed. "So, what's the latest doc?" Sheldon tried to be calm.

"Her condition deteriorated further since I last spoke with you … however, with continued treatment, her situation could change. Even so, I cannot approve of travel—not now." Sheldon's heart sank.

When the conversation with Dr. Lee had ended, Sheldon held the receiver for a long moment.

The Suite was still dark; he had not yet turned the lamps on. So he sat in the dark and pondered for a while. Then the intercom phone rang.

It was the Concierge. "Mr. Morgan, will you be placing an order for dinner, Sir."

"No, thank you, Sam; I had a big lunch. Instead, I will have fresh coffee from the Café."

Dusk had set in; Sheldon looked out through the bay window, one hand resting on the window ledge, the other holding a Bourbon drink. He watched the headlights of traffic zooming back and forth on yonder 403 highway, cars on the side roads below slow-rolled up to specified stop signs, and people walking along the sidewalk absorbing the tail-end of the warm weather. The coffee shop's Patio on the corner was bustling with customers.

He considered the inevitable realities he must face concerning Blossom's deteriorating state, and he mentally braced himself to meet her at *Ethica Mature Lifestyles* in the morning. Then, he let out a scream that echoed throughout the Suite. There was a knock on the door.

"Sir, I brought your fresh coffee…are you okay? I heard a scream coming from your Suite as I approached," said Sam.

"I am okay," Sheldon said, grateful that someone had heard him yell.

The following morning Sheldon showered and dressed. He had a restless night; he was groggy. Nevertheless, he went to the nearby café for toast and coffee. The gathering in the café was a mix of neighborhood people. The table by the window near the fireplace was where Sheldon had often sat with Blossom; this time, he sat alone. Sheldon stared at his coffee until it turned cold.

He had planned to visit Blossom by noon and have lunch with her. Up to that point, he had not gathered enough courage to tell her Dr. Lee had forbidden him to take her back to Montego Bay. He sat in the cafe for what seemed like forever.

Visions of the way life had been with Blossom and fantasies of what life ought to be, from now on, would be completely different. So maybe it was time to acknowledge what life and everyone around him had been saying. But first, he had to recognize the fears that bombarded him, and he was not ready. It was well past noon.

He went back to Suite 2108. He phoned *Ethica Mature Lifestyles*.

"Hello, Moira; how is Mrs. Morgan?"

"She's in good spirits, Mr. Morgan—I picked out a few volumes off the bookshelf from her favorite authors, and she's been reading until you get here."

Sheldon felt like saying, *I am a sad man, my heart and soul won't let me see her in her condition*, but instead, he said, "Thank you, Moira."

Sheldon felt isolated, alone with every decision he would make from now on; no point in retelling his thoughts and feelings to Gordon Rusk, Dr. Lee, or anyone else, for these moments belonged to him, and he would face them in his way.

.

CHAPTER TWO

Love gives naught but itself and takes naught but from itself.
Love possesses not nor would it be possessed;
For love is sufficient unto love.
But if in your thought you must measure time into seasons, let each season encircle all the other seasons, And let today embrace the past with remembrance and the future with longing
—*Kahlil Gibran,* The Prophet

Ethica Mature Lifestyles

It was Thursday; Blossom woke up at eight in the morning. Miles of sunshine stretched across the landscape; blue skies and fluffy, white clouds completed the setting; it was a beautiful day.

That day, neither Dr. Lee, Blossom's physician, nor Gordon Rusk, her attorney, were scheduled to visit her. Instead, she expected a visit or a phone call from Sheldon. And when a phone call came, both Moira and Blossom were over the moon with joy.

Moira Roach, the 28-year-old graduate nurse from McMaster, was assigned to Blossom's side 24/7. Moira's chair was next to Blossom's recliner by the huge window. Respectfully, she listened to stories about happier times in Blossom's life.

"My father was the leader of a Reggae Band—he played the saxophone," Blossom told Moira during story time. Mostly, Moira loved it when Blossom recited Khalil Gibran, one of her favorite authors. Moira heard a story every day about Blossom's husband, Sheldon Morgan, for her to have decided he was the most wonderful man anyone would ever meet.

"Any regrets, Mrs. Morgan? Moira asked her during Storytime.

"Yes, I regret the loss of my son."

"I wish I could step into your life story and change it, make things okay. Still, I envy your life story, though the ending is not ideal."

"The ending will be ideal when I am safely back in Sheldon's arms.."

" You are a hopeless romantic, Mrs. Morgan," Moira said and laughed sweetly.

Mrs. Evans, the director at *Ethica Mature Lifestyles*, said Sheldon alluded to becoming sad for many days after a conversation with Blossom, even though he wrote her a love letter every week. Blossom enjoyed reading Sheldon's letters.

Blossom's hairdresser Jacques came at 9 to shampoo and style her hair. Sheldon loved to see her hair brushed back and resting on her shoulders. Jacques would make sure of that. Sheldon loved her olive green raglan sleeve dress, custom-made by her Toronto dress designer.

Her silver toeless flats would go well with the olive green dress. Sheldon had given her a delicate platinum necklace with a diamond-studded cross; she would wear it with the matching diamond stud earrings.

Moira prepared Blossom to receive her beloved husband on the day in question, though, in her heart, she knew he might not come. Blossom sat in her wheelchair by the vast window and waited for Sheldon to enter her Suite. She had no clue that Dr. Lee had informed Sheldon, and Mrs. Evans, that she would not be well enough to leave or even return to Montego Bay with her husband.

Still, Sheldon insisted on having lunch with Blossom and spending the afternoon with her, even though it would be best to postpone his visit.

Blossom believed her husband would arrive late morning for brunch, and afterward, they would both leave *Ethica Mature Lifestyles*. So she was prepared to go, finally!

Moira was anxious. If Sheldon decided to show up at *Ethica*, Blossom would not let him leave without her, and he would not want to leave her. Cooler heads concluded that a face-to-face meeting between the two would leave them in great pain.

Back in suite 2108, Sheldon received updates from Michael Dixon, and that was all he could stand, at that moment, to ease his troubled mind.

"Are you listening, Boss?"

"Keep on talking, Dixon; I'm listening."

"So, two backhoes are out of service until we receive the parts to repair them; the telephone lines were down all morning, and Peggy felt like a fish out of water. When your dentist called to remind you about your appointment, Peggy had already left for the day—luckily, I was at the office, and I took the call and confirmed your appointment."

"The dentist appointment is not top of mind for me, Dixon," Sheldon said. Finally, they said goodbye and hung the phones up.

A drink of Bourbon would make him sleep. But, instead, Sheldon stared out the bay window and wondered if Blossom was resting comfortably. He, himself, would not sleep that night. It must have been past midnight, for all the lights at the gas station below were off. Blossom's slide into a life-ending condition transformed his thinking in a way he never thought possible.

When he married Blossom, he pledged to be with her until the 12th of Never, but her deteriorated state turned his guts over and fucked up his brains—Sheldon dabbed his eyes; he had abandoned the woman he loved.

He laid back in his chair. He would leave for Montego Bay in the morning, but there was no getting away from the situation that confronted him. He refused to sleep, fearing he might wake up to shocking news.

Life had given him more wealth than he asked for and had taken from him his son and the perfect health of his wife; the beautiful image of Blossom when he last saw her still stamped in his memory.

Sheldon stayed awake until dawn; he packed the minimum amount of things he needed to carry and pulled his luggage to the front door. He would be returning to Montego Bay with a heavy heart. Finally, he fell asleep with the TV on; the phone's ring startled him out of a well-needed snooze at around six.   "Sir, this is your wake-up call. You have to get to Pearson Airport; your plane leaves at ten.

"Thank you, Mason; I will be at the Rotunda in thirty minutes. He showered, dressed in jeans and a sweater, and caught the elevator to the lobby; Mason waited for Sheldon with the Ferrari running and a hot cup of coffee. Sheldon relished the coffee.

"I see you're driving my Ferrari, Mason."

"You mentioned last time that you prefer the Ferrari's ride, Mr. Morgan."

"Right you are, Mason."

.

CHAPTER THREE

"My grandfather started this construction business with his brothers a long time ago—I will not let you cut in and take what is rightfully our family's original idea." So said Doug Williams, the CEO of rival Williams Construction Company.

"It's not about your grandfather's construction business; it's about your inability to run your business efficiently," Sheldon said candidly.

"For your information, I have no plans to back away from advancing my company into the earthmoving industry just because you run your family's business poorly. One more thing, Doug Williams, if it is your idea that someone wants to take over your business, look over your shoulders at Morris Preston, your project manager. There's only one way for me, my friend, and that way is forward, so I'll get on with my life as I see fit and remain independently wealthy."

Sixty-five-year-old Sheldon Jason Morgan is a successful businessman. A Jamaican millionaire who made a fortune by expanding his earthmoving and construction company within the lucrative bauxite industry of Jamaica.

Sheldon's rise to notoriety and wealth is due to his zeal for hard work and being in the right place at the right time. His skill at operating earthmoving equipment became evident on the site of an American bauxite mining company. He extended his reach to quite a few drilling locations quickly, and his business became competitive with longstanding Williams Construction.

Sheldon is not a man for workouts because his daily activities allow the exercises he needs to maintain his lean muscular physique. His medium bronze skin tone reflects in the sunlight. His dimpled chin, evenly arched brows, pronounced laugh lines, and beautifully set teeth—barely visible through his artfully coiffed mustache—are attributes he took for granted. When his hairline receded, he shaved his head and maintained a bald look. He is a tough man with rippled arms that could bruise a woman's skin, yet Sheldon never considers himself overtly alluring.

When Sheldon was a young man, he enrolled in Theological College but dropped out of seminary shortly afterward. However, he promised his father he would learn a trade and make something of himself.

"Son, since you quit theology, you ought to learn a trade. I'll speak to my friend George Fairweather and see if he'll take you on as an apprentice in his construction business."

Sheldon was bent on pleasing his father. He was the man who taught Sheldon the Cricket game and introduced him to the music of trumpeter Miles Davis. But most of all, he held Sheldon's hand each morning during his walk to school.

George Fairweather was a friend of Sheldon's father. He mentored and trained young Sheldon in road work. Sheldon learned well under the teaching of Fairweather, so in later years when George Fairweather became ill and shaky, Shelton grabbed the opportunity to purchase his shop for a little more than nothing. And his father rewarded him with a fully paid four-year college education in civil engineering.

Thelma Morgan, Sheldon's mother, was who he went to for advice, counsel, and all things spiritual. She expected Sheldon to be all she wanted him to be and hoped Sheldon would continue the church mission she started; instead, he veered to a different route, which was not her liking.

Thelma considered herself a woman of importance. Everyone called her Mother Morgan when she established a holiness church in the community; no one would dare call her by her first name *Thelma*. The famous preacher lady at the holiness church was Mother Morgan to people in the district; even the priest at the Anglican church, where her parents were regular Parishioners, envied the enormous size of her gatherings. Her worship place aptly named, The Shed.

The Shed, constructed with board siding and zinc top, was the common meeting place for gospel seekers, and even when it turned into a brick-and-mortar structure, people still called it The Shed.

Thelma's teenage life was disturbing to the people in the district. At sixteen years old, people thought she had suddenly disappeared from the neighborhood. The truth was, her parents promptly sent her away, to a place no one knew, except her parents, when they discovered she was with child. She stayed out of sight for two years and returned to the community with a toddler. Her return was not without arguments and idle chatter by town gossipers, especially about the actual connections of the toddler. The toddler, a male child, sat quietly in an oblong wicker basket as Thelma preached about her enlightened state and a Savior to passersby. Thelma's youth and knowledge about the bible attracted big Sunday afternoon crowds. However, it was not until she was twenty-one that she became the wife of Audley Morgan, a neighborhood young man who fell in love with her and adored her little boy.

As far back as Sheldon remembered, his mother had been a preacher. Sheldon followed his mother to preaching engagements during his younger years, preached at her open-air meetings, and studied the bible at her feet. Sheldon was indeed his father's son and the apple of his mother's eye. His ways attracted women considered upper class, even if his religion was different than theirs, and they flocked to his mother's meetings to witness Sheldon's charismatic presentations. But, of course, Sheldon would not acknowledge that any trace of narcissism on his part was an outgrowth from his mother's ordeal at 16 and her inflated sense of herself.

Sheldon Morgan is who people call an introvert. He rarely participates in the activities of high-powered executives; he prefers to work hard and is often seen operating a backhoe on his construction sites or hanging out with his workers; instead of being at expensive bars and upscale clubs. Still, work is a significant part of his life at his age, even though he has all the help he needs to hire.

CHAPTER FOUR

For even as he ascends to your height and caresses your tenderest branches that quiver in the sun,
So shall he descend to your roots and shake them in their clinging to the earth.
—*Kahlil Gibran,* The Prophet

The flight back to Montego Bay from Toronto was harrowing, mainly because Sheldon spent the entire time lamenting over not bringing Blossom back home. He was itching to request another drink of rum and Coke from the flight attendant making the rounds, but instead, he asked for a black coffee without sugar. Sheldon felt like he had abandoned Blossom. Even as he had packed his bags to leave Suite 2108, he did not feel strong enough to tell Blossom he was on his way back to Montego Bay; he closed his eyes and said a prayer in flight.

Dear God,
My heart is pressing on my soul
Take this heart of mine and give me a strong heart
Give me a heart that relies on your mercy; a heart that can endure
And forgive my sinful self
Dear God, please make my wife well again
Give her one more chance at a healthy life
Bring her home to me; place her in my arms
Is my prayer, and so be it.

Dixon was waiting for Sheldon at the airport pickup curb. The two men greeted each other; Sheldon slid into the passenger seat of the SUV; and buckled his seat belt. Dixon noticed his sulk and decided against inquiring about his flight, which he usually did when he greeted Sheldon on returning home from a trip. Finally, they reached Sheldon's residence, "Thank you, Dixon," he said and waved.

Sheldon's decision not to visit Blossom before leaving troubled him as he prepared for bed. He lay in the darkness mulling over the past week's events and wondering what he might have done differently. His decision not to see Blossom before leaving *Ethica Mature Lifestyles* had his head reeling. He regretted that he had to leave her. Finally, in the wee hours of the morning, he fell asleep.

At sunrise, he awoke dazed from a lack of sleep. He determined a shower and hot black coffee would perk up his listless body. He sorted and replied to a pile of mail on his desk in his study. Among the letters was a letter from Odette Black, the Town Mayor and sister of Blossom, imploring him to enter the race for a seat in Jamaica's parliament.

"You are honest, you understand the people in our community, and you are compassionate; you'd represent us well as a member of parliament." She wrote in her note.

Sheldon had discussed the idea with Blossom, but with her ill health on his mind, he knew he had made the right decision when he said no to the request. He opened a letter from Blossom. The fragrance of lavender emanated from the folds; the writing paper was a soft pink.

My darling Sheldon
After all this time, I love you still.
Your true love, Bloss.

The temperature outside was already warm; it would turn out to be a sweltering day.

Peggy called, "Attorney Jones will be in Court today to settle compensation matters regarding the two workplace accidents a year ago."

"Thank you, Peggy; I had forgotten the cases would finalize today."

"And Roy's fencing is coming in to secure the border around the parking area at West Hill site."

"Is the Electricity back on, and all is well?" Sheldon asked.

"Yes, Sir, electricity and phones have been back since yesterday afternoon."

Sheldon was pleased with Peggy's update. He

picked up his pen:

Dear Bloss,
I spent some time in the rose garden early this morning. The yellow roses you planted bloomed again; I cut six long stems and put them in an urn on our bedside table.
Darling, I am at my wit's end; I don't know how to live without you. You have given me the best years of my life; the laughter and the tears of joy in intimate moments have been stamped indelibly on my heart.
I did not come to see you at Ethica, and you knew why. You knew I could not stand to see you the way you have become. I want to remember you as my beautiful Bloss. The woman whose breasts I hunger for. It warms my heart, knowing your love is tied to me and mine to you. See you soon. Sheldon.

At the sound of the long-distance ring tone, Sheldon turned his head to the clock on the wall. He inhaled deeply. A long-distance ring tone made him anxious about what he might hear, especially at that hour.

"Hello? It is you, Dixon. Where the hell are you calling from?"

"Kingston, Boss, the Labor Union tribunal is today."

"The boys are back on the job at West Hill. I understand"….Sheldon trailed off

"Yes, Sir, Peggy and lawyer Jones's office will take care of the documents," Dixon said.

To say Michael Dixon was Sheldon's right-hand

man would not be sufficient. Dixon had been in Sheldon's employ for two decades. He operated every equipment on the worksites and was the reference point when Sheldon needed someone to chip in. Sheldon trusted Dixon. He was a true company man; he appreciated Dixon's loyalty.

When Sheldon made Dixon the Project Manager, his workers developed sore eyes. But Dixon became a brother who cared about all aspects of Sheldon's life, and when Dixon married Millie, Sheldon had an instant sister.

Sheldon grabbed the keys to his GMC truck and walked out the door. He drove out to the West Hill site, prepared to operate an available backhoe if necessary. Instead, standing on the mound near a giant dugout, he observed equipment operators loading oversize trucks with bauxite ore to haul away. The operation was running like a well-oiled machine.

On his way back to his residence, it was already lunchtime; he planned to stop at Cool Runnings Bar and Grill, his place to release pent-up stress. Customers who frequented Cool Runnings came from the area's bauxite mining industry, old-school reggae music enthusiasts, and diners hungry for authentic traditional dishes.

Suddenly, Sheldon's had a mind to phone Blossom at *Ethica Mature Lifestyles*.

"Mrs. Morgan is taking her afternoon nap, Mr. Morgan," Moira said. Sheldon was unsure if he should feel relieved; he motored on to Cool Runnings. He walked in, pulled up a chair at the counter, and ordered bottled water. He surveyed the afternoon lunch crowd.

The aged proprietor, affectionately named *Sexy*, who Blossom called *Uncle Sexy*, had been a member of Blossom's father's Reggae band. *Sexy* ambled over to Sheldon. "Glad to see you, Mr. Sheldon; how are you today, Sir?"

"I am well, *Sexy*. Is your knee acting up again?"

"Need to get a walking cane, Mr. Sheldon."

Sheldon's eyes caught Tony Wilson, Plant Manager from a nearby Factory, and beckoned him over. "Hungry?—I ordered wings—jerk chicken wings—eat some with me."

Tony saw the worry in his colleague's eyes; he could tell that Sheldon's troubles were concerning his ill wife in Canada, and he wished he could help him to find peace. "Sure, Sheldon, I'll have some jerk chicken wings." Tony shook his head from side to side.

"Want to go boating with me afterward?"

"Sure, pal."

Sheldon's friends, Ford and Julius, had been at Cool Runnings for lunch, and they went with Sheldon and Tony for a fun afternoon boat ride.

CHAPTER FIVE

"Scotch on the rocks for the king of the hill, Red Stripe beers for the underlings, and jerk chicken wings for all of us." So said Julius, followed by an extended bout of laughter from the other men.

They returned to Cool Runnings for drinks and chatted after their boating jaunt. The four of them sat at a square table by the window. The Band was on stage; *Sexy* played the drums with a group from his old reggae Band.

Night had fallen. The day had sped by quickly. Sheldon and his friends were jovial. Concerned as Sheldon was about Blossom's condition, he calmed down as best he could to put his friends at ease. Julius beckoned the waitress. "We're starving over here; how much longer do we wait?"

"A hungry man is an angry man," Tony cut in. Shortly after, the server came with the drinks and wings; Julius paid with a generous tip; the men clinked their glasses and drank slow sips. Then, suddenly, someone said, "Gentlemen!"

Doug Williams was staring at them with a drink in his hand, wanting to join in.

"Hey, Doug, grab a seat," Sheldon was polite.

Doug Williams' interruption was to announce the sale of used backhoes.

"My friend, Douce, at the East Hill site, is selling two old backhoes; I plan to purchase them for spare parts," Doug said.

"Good for you, man; I recently purchased new spare parts in Toronto."

"Excavation will wear out the equipment, I tell you." Doug went on.

Sheldon switched the subject. "I am sorry that my lawyer was rough with your lawyer the other day in court, man, but your workers won't stop stealing parts from my equipment yard."

"You are right, Sheldon; their actions are costly in the end." After that, the men chatted about things in general. Sheldon was happy to forget his worries, if only for a short while. Ford kept track of time; he announced in a pleasant tone, "Tomorrow is another day, men; we should leave now." So they parted to their respective vehicles and drove away.

The housekeeper, Caroline, was working in the kitchen the following morning, which woke Sheldon up at precisely five o'clock. Rest had escaped him the night before. He chucked the body pillow he had been hugging; it landed in the bedroom recliner like a useless lump; more than anything, Sheldon desired his wife alongside him.

He slung one leg over the side of the bed and then the next and dashed to the adjacent bathroom for a cold shower. The warm breeze that flowed through the louver enveloped him; as he dressed in blue jeans and a button-down powder-blue long sleeves shirt. He descended the winding mahogany wood stairs to the open kitchen overlooking the rose garden. He could tell it would be a warm day.

Sheldon heard footsteps coming from the backyard. "Good morning Mr. Sheldon." Millie had been tending the rose garden. Millie, along with Blossom, had kept the gardens in tiptop shape.

"Good morning, Millie. Did Dixon shove you out of bed this early morning?" Sheldon asked with a laugh.

"No, Sir, I am tending the rose garden and the vegetable patch today."

Breakfast was the same every morning, three eggs over easy, crispy bacon, two slices of toast, and black coffee. He liked his breakfast a certain way, and he made it himself. Then, before he ate, he repeated the same long mantra to cover the eventualities of the day. Caroline, the housekeeper, knew not to interrupt his morning routine.

At around six o'clock that morning, Sheldon answered the phone. "Damn it, Dixon; I am in the middle of breakfast; you know I have breakfast at this time every morning…what the hell is your problem?"

"Good morning Mr. Morgan," came the soft

voice on the phone. "This is Moira calling from *Ethica Mature Lifestyles."*

Sheldon's heart skipped several beats. He pushed his breakfast plate to the side. Calls from *Ethica* Mature Lifestyles were either with Blossom at the end of the line or from staff about Blossom. Sheldon listened to an account of Blossom's passing from Moira at the other end of the phone line, but instead, he heard the voice of Blossom reading a passage from her favorite author.

> *For what is it to die but to stand naked in the wind and to melt into the sun?*
> *And what is it to cease breathing, but to free the breath from its restless tides, that it may rise and expand and seek God unencumbered?*
> *—Kahlil Gibran,* The Prophet

The news from Ethica sent chills through Sheldon's body. Suddenly he was experiencing his worst nightmare. He gripped the phone and slammed it down on the ledge; he would dial his father; then, he remembered his father had been incoherent with Alzheimer's disease. He shook his head vigorously to recall his mother's telephone number, no need; she's been gone a few years. "God," Sheldon said aloud, "help me, please."

Confused as he had been, Sheldon recognized he was at that point where he could endure for Blossom's sake—be the strength on which she had depended.

Caroline and Millie huddled on the other side

of the sliding doors; they could tell something serious had happened. Sheldon's gaze led him out the sliding doors to the Patio. He leaned against the railings and watched the sunrise, to pass the time away.

His assistant Peggy will be in the office at 8.30 a.m. "Good morning, Peggy; book me on the next flight out of Sangster's Airport to Pearson in Toronto."

"Certainly, Sir," Peggy knew not to probe an instruction from Sheldon; she sensed something grave had occurred. Next, Sheldon phoned Dixon. He made it clear he did not call to chat or get an update; he said, "I must be on the next flight out of Montego Bay to Toronto." Dixon paused for a brief moment. From the sound in Sheldon's voice, he could tell something serious was wrong. He was cautious.

"The Missis is gone, Boss?"

"Fuck it, Dixon, don't ask me a dumbass question—Do as you are told. And get your ass in the SUV and take me to the airport--now."

"Okay, Boss."

When Dixon answered the phone in Sheldon's home that morning, he could not believe his ears. More than two decades after Sheldon divorced her, Maureen Grant was on the phone asking to speak to Sheldon. Though Dixon had been Sheldon's Project Manager, more importantly, he was the friend Sheldon leaned on in many instances. Few people had access to Sheldon unless Michael Dixon allowed them.

"Why do you want to speak to Sheldon, Maureen?"

"Who made you gatekeeper for Sheldon?" Maureen never liked Dixon, even when she was married to Sheldon.

"He did. I am sorry, Maureen, Mr. Morgan is not available; he will be out of the country for a while; maybe I can help you," Dixon said.

Maureen sounded desperate. "I am not calling to ask Sheldon for money or anything like that," she said, recognizing she would be wise to tell Dixon why she was calling Sheldon.

"That's a good start—then, maybe I can help;" Dixon was eternally cynical about Maureen Grant.

Her life after Sheldon's hasty divorce from her was far from what she anticipated. She had married a minerals prospector from Quebec, Canada, and resided in a hifalutin neighborhood outside Kingston. Unfortunately, her husband went bankrupt, died of a heart attack, and left her penniless. In addition, Dixon never forgave Maureen for lying to Sheldon about a child she was allegedly carrying, which led to a hasty marriage and a messy divorce. Plus, Dixon knew about the verbal spats between Maureen and Blossom over Sheldon that left him taking Blossom's side. However, despite her incredibly foolish behavior, he listened to what Maureen had to say. Maureen was clever in her approach; she only talked about her mother's recent death; and the upcoming funeral.

"My Mother and Sheldon's mother were long-time friends; Sheldon knows this, and he would want to be at Mom's funeral."

Dixon would have been heartless if he had not shown sympathy.

"Sorry to hear about your mother, Maureen; I will let Mr. Morgan know—good luck." Dixon could hear Maureen saying *hello, hello* as he ended the call and hung up the phone. If Maureen were looking for personal favors from Sheldon, Dixon would not recommend it.

CHAPTER SIX

Your pain is the breaking of the shell that encloses your understanding.
Even as the stone of the fruit must break, that its heart may stand in the sun, so must you know pain.
And you would accept the seasons of your heart, even as you have always accepted the seasons that pass over your fields.
And you would watch with serenity through the winters of your grief.
—Kahlil Gibran, The Prophet

Sheldon hardly had enough time to pack his bags and be ready to leave for Toronto. Instead, he stuffed a few essentials in his carry-on luggage. "That's all I'm going to carry with me," he said to Peggy when she called with his travel arrangements. "I got you booked on an afternoon flight from here, Sir."

When he descended the stairs into the kitchen, Caroline and Millie were sitting on the Patio; both women had been crying; neither one of them spoke.

Dixon picked up Sheldon's luggage from the hallway and carried them to the SUV. He had a weary look in his eyes. Sheldon followed after him, sat in the passenger's seat, and buckled his seat belt.

"Caroline," Millie said, wiping a tear, "Let us go tend Miss Bloss' rose garden."

Dixon turned the SUV onto the main road heading to the airport; the traffic was free-flowing. Visibility was good despite the early morning fog. Sheldon sat stiffly, staring forward, wondering if he should give up his pride and tell Dixson how scared he was; he grunted. Dixon looked sideways at him; "You okay, Boss?" Dixon was concerned. Sheldon groaned one more time. He was reeling from the shocking news he had received from *Ethica Mature Lifestyles*.

Thanks to Peggy's pre-arrangements, Sheldon cleared customs in record time and settled in the lounge area; he had avoided the line-up confusion. Once he entered the lounge, Dixon pointed him to a round table with two chairs. They sat quietly.

"May I get you some tea, Boss?"

"Thank you, Dixon—Earl Gray, no sugar," a slight smile brightened Sheldon's face.

Dixon pulled his chair closer. "Boss, I say this as a friend, not an employee; you have endured a lot since Miss Bloss became ill. She has been your life, and now you have lost your life. But like a cat, you have nine lives, Sir, you will survive; go, see to your wife's interment, and come back stronger, nonetheless."

"Dixon," Sheldon paused, "my beloved wife will no longer be with me … I do not know how to deal with the situation … I am searching."

Dixon shook his head side to side; he knew the moment called for silence. We waited for Sheldon to speak; Sheldon remained silent. Finally, Dixon rose, shook Sheldon's hand, and left. Sheldon looked at his watch, stood up, and proceeded on board.

During the flight out of Montego Bay, memories of him and Blossom put smiles on his face. He recalled the heavy rainstorm long ago. Blossom had been standing at an overcrowded bus stop. He pulled up alongside the shelter; *"Miss Black, may I offer you a lift?"* he had said to Blossom, who had been standing in the crammed bus shelter. She had looked at him with suspicious eyes.

"Hop in quickly." He had said, worried that his old, banged-up, black Chevrolet van would run out of gasoline soon.

"Hi, my name is Sheldon Morgan." He could see she was relaxing. He tried to make her feel safe by telling her he had been a student at the same school as she and knew her teacher as Miss White.

He had noticed her outstanding features: long black hair, beautiful green eyes, and light brown skin.

Blossom wanted to know about the courses he studied. He liked her curiosity. Blossom liked that he worked in construction when he told her he operated heavy equipment on the highway construction project near Montego Bay; Sheldon's windshield wiper blades conked out during the rainstorm, and she scolded him. Then, when he reached her home, the passenger side door of his truck stuck; she lost her footing on stepping out and fell into Sheldon's arms. Their lips met in a brief kiss, and he knew the gods were kind to him, even during that rainstorm.

The pilot announced that the plane had reached cruise level. Sheldon loosened his seatbelt and laid his head back. The magnitude of the pain he would bear over the loss of Blossom and how different being alone in their home would be was overwhelming. His thoughts about the times he and Blossom talked and laughed as they reclined in the rose garden, how she laughed at his silly jokes, and how she yielded to his touch when he made love to her was more than he could bear.

Few people knew the personality of Blossom Black, the woman Sheldon affectionately named Bloss. They took her at face value; saw her as egotistical and snobbish. But Sheldon was familiar with Blossom's adventurous nature, how she accepted life and rode with opportunities and ever-changing situations. Blossom had relentless willpower, great self-discipline, and an excellent work ethic, and Sheldon yielded to her charisma in every way.

Now, more than ever, he wished he had a shoulder on which to cry. But unfortunately, his parents were no longer available to him. His mother, the pastor he adored and leaned on her every word, had died five years earlier. He often wondered if the religious route he avoided would have served him well in his grief. Sheldon hailed the flight attendant who was making the rounds. "Rum and Coke, please—with ice cubes."

The account of his son, his only child, was a guilty memory; he felt responsible for the aftermath of his reckless arranged meeting with Blossom while he was yet married to Maureen Grant.

The mating call was loud; Sheldon was calling, and Blossom was already answering. She rushed ahead along the passageway, past the sitting area, and into their Suite. She barely made it to the chaise. Sheldon was in pursuit. He could not have made it any farther than the chaise lounge.

Blossom presented herself to Sheldon with no reservations, and he took her without regrets. They laid back on the sofa cushions that lined the chase, not moving, not speaking, feeling as one with each other, and loving the silent communion.
— CRY TOUGH

The aftermath of that moment would bother both of them for the rest of their life.

A year had passed. Sheldon's slap-dash marriage to Maureen Grant had steadily deteriorated; Blossom had produced a son.

When Sheldon and Maureen arrived at Pearson Airport en route to Niagara Falls for a vacation, Sheldon's curiosity led him to seek out Blossom. He telephoned her from the airport, but instead of a cordial response, he heard the story about a secret child he fathered with her, and said child succumbed to SIDS. Shock propelled Sheldon to a small church in Etobicoke. He noticed Blossom kneeling beside a tiny coffin at the altar. She had been weeping.

Blossom and David Clark, her husband, walked hand in hand past him, to the exit door at the back of the church, without a mere glance in his direction.

Sheldon did not fully understand it; how could fate have taken his child and brought Blossom back to him in such a big way? But even as fate made both of them pay, inflicting an illness on Blossom, this was the last straw.

"Ladies and gentlemen, as we start our descent, please ensure your seat backs and tray tables are fully upright. Also, ensure your seat belt is securely fastened, and all carry-on luggage is stowed underneath the seat in front of you or the overhead bins. Thank you."

The plane sloped down. Sheldon fastened his seatbelt for landing at Toronto Pearson airport.

Gordon Rusk, Sheldon's attorney, was leaning against his Mercedes Benz when Sheldon stepped out by the side of the pickup curb. So was Mason, Sheldon's Chauffeur. They had come to receive him; Sheldon was happy to see them both. First, he exchanged remarks with both men. Then, before Sheldon went and sat in the passenger side of his Ferrari for the ride to his Suite in Building Two of the Emerald Towers, he said to Gordon, "I'll see you in the meeting room at Tower Two in thirty minutes."

As soon as Sheldon dropped his luggage in suite 2108, he proceeded to the meeting room to meet with Gordon. They talked about funeral arrangements for Blossom.

"The Funeral directors have planned the event from beginning to end—every aspect of it," Gordon Rusk assured Sheldon.

"You pay me well, Mr. Morgan, but more than that, Mrs. Morgan was a good friend to me; it is an honor to take some of the burdens of this challenging period off you." Gordon continued.

"You've been a big help, Gordon."

The men shook hands and said goodnight. Sheldon entered an elevator to the 21st floor. He expected it to be a long sleepless night. And though he felt a burden, it was not weighty.

When Sheldon entered Suite 2108, the red light on his answering phone was glaring. He listened in and deleted messages. Among the voice messages was one from Dixon saying he had called to check if Sheldon's *faculties* were still intact. Sheldon smiled—just like Dixon to be humorous. A cup of Chamomile was what he needed before he reclined in Blossom's chair.

The following morning Sheldon woke up at seven from a short nap; a fire truck zipped along the street below; traffic built up along the 403 highway, and the Café's open light blinked on.

He showered, dressed, and exited Building Two for a twenty-minute walk around the block. The wind that greeted him when he opened the lobby door was sharp against his face, just what he needed to start the day. After that, it would be a day of completion.

CHAPTER SEVEN

The morning had a dreamlike feel. Sheldon Morgan arrived thirty minutes early at the small church he had sat in nearly thirty years ago for his son's funeral. He stood beside his wife's casket; there was much to reminisce about their life together. Finally, he was ready to perform the duties expected of him. Gibran resounded in his ears.

Farewell to you and the youth I have spent with you
It was, but yesterday we met in a dram
You have sung to me in my aloneness, and I of your longings, have built a tower in the sky.
If in the twilight of memory we should meet once more, we shall speak again together, and you shall sing to me a deeper song —Kahlil Gibran, The Prophet

In the Chapel
Family, friends, and colleagues of Blossom Mae Black gathered for a funeral Mass in her honor.

The low, subtle sound of the Pipe Organ filled the air in the small chapel in quaint Etobicoke, a town on the rim of the city of Toronto. Father Templeton officiated; Dana Clark, the stepdaughter of Blossom, eulogized with a poem. Sheldon sat throughout the dignified affair like a zombie.

Blossom Black, a sophisticated woman, displayed her style one last time. Sheldon looked at his wife's body before the casket closed, and he was pleased. Her final wishes were as she requested. The closed casket, the center of attraction near the pulpit, typified the home of Blossom Mae Black. Despite Sheldon's extraordinary alertness, the moment's reality had left him speechless.

The day ended with a party of six, dining at the home of Daisy Ivanov. Daisy Ivanov's husband, John, a Russian man, was one of Blossom's philanthropic friends; he shared Blossom's kindness and compassion to battered women and homeless men. Daisy served Beef Stroganoff with pasta, steamed green beans, and a crisp side salad for dinner. Sheldon enjoyed the Russian fare. Lighthearted anecdotes with great humor made the after-dinner chatter delightful. It was nine when Sheldon left the home of the Ivanovs. Mason had been waiting in the Ferrari to take him home.

"The night is relatively calm, Mr. Morgan," Mason said once Sheldon settled in the passenger seat and buckled up. But, despite Mason's observation, Sheldon knew calm would not let him rest.

Mason stopped at the curb just outside Tower

Two of the Emerald Towers. "Good night Mr. Morgan," he said and drove off to park the Ferrari.

The following day at five o'clock evening time, Blossom's relatives, close friends, and colleagues gathered at Mill restaurant for the scheduled dinner party in her memory. The small, elaborate affair came off how Blossom had designed it before she departed. Dinner was exquisitely prepared; tasty hors d'oeuvres were passed around lavishly, expensive champagne flowed into glass flutes, and the Band played Blossom's favorite songs. Blossom's stepdaughters, Dana and Camile Clark were in attendance. In addition, her sister, Odette Black, and two of Odette's sons arrived from Montego Bay. Her brother, Boyd Stephenson, from Cleveland, Ohio, had phoned Sheldon to say his plane from Chicago O'Hare airport would be late by an hour. When he arrived with his beautiful wife and teenage daughter, the group in the reception room at the Mill applauded.

It was noticeable when famed criminal defense attorney Ron Johnson walked into the room in drunken strides. He sat at the head table between Gordon Rusk and Sheldon Morgan.

"Greetings to both of you," he said, looking from one man to the next. Both men nodded. Then he glanced sideways, "Hello, Father Templeton; Mrs. Templeton." Mrs. Templeton smiled, and Father Templeton nodded.

Father Templeton was at his priestly self; all dressed in regalia. He rose and walked to the mike, pulled a folded sheet from his side pocket, and began his speech with a biblical quote:

For now, we see in a mirror, darkly, but then face to face. Now I know in part, but then I shall know just as I also am known.

People stepped up to the mike to tell stories about the life they experienced with Blossom. Some stories brought tears, but most brought laughter. Ron Johnson staggered up to the mike; he delivered his speech like a performance before a Magistrate. Gordon Rusk held a long breath until Ron Johnson finished his over-the-top oratory.

"You know how Ron is glib—one never knows what he might say under difficult circumstances, and this is one of those circumstances," Gordon whispered to Sheldon.

"I am no longer surprised about Ron," Sheldon whispered back.

One of the best criminal defense attorneys among his peers, Ron Johnson, had been more than a close friend of Blossom; he had been a lover who competed with Sheldon Morgan for Blossom's heart. He hated Sheldon and sparred with Blossom because of her relationship with Sheldon. Ron Johnson had hoped his fame and wealth would bring Blossom back to him, if not her affection, and the twenty-five-year rivalry continued between Ron Johnson and Sheldon Morgan.

"It's that idiot son-of-a-bitch in Montego Bay you call Sheldon, isn't it? It's him. That mother fucker ... wherever he is, I'm going to hunt him down and pound the son-of-a-bitch to a bloody pulp. So Ron had said when Blossom announced she was carrying a child.

Ron staggered back to the head table, where he sat with Gordon Rusk and Sheldon Morgan. "Man, you are handling this thing better than I could...I applaud you." He said to Sheldon.

Sheldon considered responding to Ron; *You, Sir, are a man whose jaw I would gladly punch for having the nerve to show up in a drunken state at my wife's funeral reception.*

But Sheldon straightened up and walked to the mike; all the time, he was thinking about Blossom. Then, he began to speak, *"Over the years, we have done so much together; every day with you was something new. I'm so grateful that we shared our lives; Bloss, you trusted me, you were a faithful friend, a true lover, and I could count on you to follow through. You were my life. When I lost you, I lost my life."*

Sheldon would not say he was at peace with the loss of his wife; he never would. But he was at ease knowing he had given her all, and she had poured her love on him. Sheldon stepped away from the mike; he looked around the room; there was no dry eye. Then, Mrs. Phillips, a dear friend of Blossom and a resident at *Ethica Mature lifestyles,* stepped into Sheldon's presence. "Mr. Morgan, I am truly sorry for your loss, Mrs. Morgan; she was a friend to me" Mrs. Phillips paused to dab her eyes. "When I lost my husband Fred fifteen years ago, I thought I'd die—I'm still standing. My consolation is you will manage; your wife demands it of you." "Thank you, Mrs. Phillips; you reminded me my wife would have wanted me to manage."

Ron Johnson was sulking over Blossom's passing; Sheldon conversed with Gordon Rusk at the barrier alongside the dining room; attendees mingled. Then, suddenly, Ron walked up, pointed an index finger at Sheldon, and said, "You, Sheldon Morgan, have taken Blossom from me at the apex of our love, and I hate you for that; I've always wanted to bloody your nose, and I will do it now…." Ron raised a fist.

Sheldon slapped Ron's fist away, lurching him over tables. He sprawled on the floor to the sound of oohs and aahs from concerned guests. Sheldon pulled Ron up from the floor, brushed off his lapel, and straightened his tie. Then he took Ron's car keys away and called a taxi to take him home.

After that, the mood in the room turned lively. Gordon Rusk and Odette Black were engaged in conversation. Boyd Stephenson had an arm around his wife's shoulders. The servers came with more champagne and cocktail snacks; Sheldon signaled the Band to strike up a rhythm he knew Blossom liked; everyone danced to the *Macarena*.

Gordon Rusk teased Sheldon when the gathering fanned out, "You tried to kill Ron Johnson at the Reception tonight, I see…." He trailed off. Sheldon continued the humor, "He'll be fine, Gordon;

remember that no good deed goes unpunished." The two men chuckled.

It was a triumphant finale to the exciting life of Blossom Mae Black. Despite Ron Johnson, Sheldon thanked Gordon for helping him through the day.

CHAPTER EIGHT

The view from the sunroom in Suite 2108 was exceptional; Sheldon could see the top of the CN Tower glistening in the sunlight. The apartment was quiet except for a low hum coming from the air conditioner. The previous days' activities were still fresh. Suddenly Sheldon experienced the peace of mind that eluded him for quite some time.

Sheldon would spend the entire morning replying to sympathy notes and acknowledging sentiments on behalf of his wife. He was grateful for the support that friends and colleagues had shown. The phone rang as he was about to rise and make lunch.

"Hello, Mr. Morgan, Boyd Stephenson, here; Jess and I want to say goodbye before we return to Chicago; we request you have dinner with us."

"I would love it, Boyd; I know a charming restaurant at the foot of Lakeshore Road—it is a cozy place; Blossom and I were patrons—I hope you don't mind my choosing the restaurant."

"No, not at all; I was secretly hoping you would; I am unfamiliar with this city."

"Then I will make dinner reservations for tomorrow at 6."

"Excellent, Sheldon, excellent!"

Sheldon hesitated for a minute before putting the receiver back on its base. Except at the celebratory gathering for Blossom, he had only met Boyd Stephenson two times when he and his family vacationed in Montego Bay. And although he agreed on dinner with Boyd Stephenson and his wife, his sixth sense warned him about undercurrents. Sheldon understood; family niceties, but at what cost? He would be cautious.

It had rained the following morning heavily. Mason had a doctor's appointment, so Sheldon went by train to Toronto Union Station and walked the short distance to the Harbour Castle Hotel, where he and Gordon had pre-meeting lunch reservations.

Sheldon lounged in the lobby with legs crossed at the ankle while waiting for Gordon to arrive. He glanced around, thinking how attractive the place was; the entire ambiance was pleasing. And while he admired the beautiful prints on the wall, Gordon approached with an outstretched arm for a handshake.

"Come along, fellow... let us have lunch—can't wait to stick my knife and fork into the mouthwatering rib-eye steak they serve here." Both men walked in stride into the dining room. They sat down to eat; Gordon ordered the fare; Sheldon paid the bill.

"You've held up well, I see."

"The only way to go, Gordon."

"I heard from Boyd Stephenson," said Gordon in-between mouthfuls. "He inquired about potential work at the firm, and I told him I might consider a request with your endorsement."

"That could be one reason he asks for dinner with me; however, if he mentions such considerations, I will bounce the ball back into your Court. But, of course, I will not be pleased to see Blossom's half-brother employed in the firm that holds her legal dossier."

"You can count on me to poo-poo his request," Gordon said, savoring his rib-eye steak.

Sheldon was matter of fact, "Gordon, I feel like my trust in you is well deserved." Gordon was pleased to hear the comment.

After lunch, the two men continue their conversation in Gordon's Office. "Work on the Chalet in Collingwood is progressing nicely." So Gordon said when they were comfortably seated in his office.

"I'm glad to hear—now is a good time to hire someone to manage the Chalet."

"By all means—I'll engage an agency to do the recruitment."

Gordon swivels his chair toward his hide-away Bar at the side of his large desk. He pulls out an unopen bottle of cognac and two wine glasses, uncork the bottle, and pour drinks. They sip—Gordon turns pages in his appointment book. Sheldon turns the Band on his ring finger, a habit he hopes to maintain for a long time. Then, suddenly, Gordon said, "Sheldon, I hired a criminal defense lawyer to lead that side of my firm's legal work.—and he is a twofer.

"How so?"

"He brought a one-time prosecutor turned criminal defense lawyer," Gordon pressed a big gold button on his desk. "Irene, I wish to speak with Mr. Montoy—send him in."

Gordon Rusk had heard about the gentleman's charisma long before meeting him. So he approached at the end of a court hearing in which they were counsels, and Gordon invited Montoy to join his Law Firm. Montoy accepted without too much persuading. He had an eye on Gordon Rusk's law firm as a jump-off point from which to launch his law office. So Gordon was not put off when his offer turned into a two-for-one. The gentleman alluded to an ongoing relationship with a former lady prosecutor whom he wished to bring to the new job.

"He assured me he would keep his relationship with this lady private."

"And I am about to meet this gentleman you talk about so highly?"

"Yes—Montoy, Jose Montoy."

Jose Montoy knocks and enters Gordon Rusk's Office. He nods politely at the individual seated in the client's chair. "Mr. Rusk, I brought Blossom Black's Estate file—there are a few things to update."

"Thank you, Mr. Montoy." Gordon Rusk pauses for a long moment, holding the file in his hand.

"You wished to speak with me, Mr. Rusk," said Montoy, referring back to the signal he got from the receptionist, Irene.

"Mr. Montoy, please meet Mr. Sheldon Morgan, the widower of Blossom Block."

Jose Montoy stretched out his hand to Sheldon; his simultaneous grin was a quick, nervous reflex action on realizing *that* Sheldon Morgan had been the man sitting in the guest chair, "I am pleased to meet you, Mr. Morgan." Said Montoy. Sheldon responded with a nod.

Finally, when Montoy left the room, Sheldon remarked, "I hope your employment of Mr. Montoy will turn out to be what your firm is looking for." Gordon nods slowly.

Then, Gordon noticed Sheldon's tired eyes. "Spend a few days at the Chalet before you return to Montego Bay—the rooms are renovated and ready to live in, and the golf course is designed for use."

Sheldon was melancholy. With Blossom's passing still on his mind, he would consider Gordon's suggestion and spend four days at the Chalet. Mason was waiting for Sheldon at the front entrance of Gordon Rusk's office building. Sheldon slid into the Ferrari and buckled his seat belt for the commute to Etobicoke.

"I hope the doctor gave you a clean bill of health," Sheldon said to Mason.

"All is well, Sir," Mason replied.

The drive back to Suite 2108 was tranquil; Sheldon asked Mason not to turn the radio on so he could reflect in total silence. Traffic on the QEW highway was unusually light. Vehicles moved at a comfortable pace.

With Mason let go for the evening, Sheldon collected his mail at the letterbox and proceeded toward the elevators.

"Have a good night, Mr. Morgan," the Concierge called out as Sheldon entered an elevator. However, before he went to sleep, Sheldon listened to phone messages. He had intended to swallow a sleeping pill to bring him to sleep until the middle of the following day, but then the phone rang. He had a mind to disregard the ring, but the sound was too loud to ignore, so he grabbed a bottle of Evian water from the refrigerator, picked up his sleeping pill, and said, "Hello, Dixon."

"How was your day, Boss?

"Doing all I can, Dixon."

"I am calling to update you."

"Couldn't the update wait?"

"No, Boss, I have excellent news you should hear tonight. Peggy got word today from Lawyer Jones that our proposal to provide work at the North region site is accepted."

"That is excellent news, Dixon. I knew I could rely on Jones to make a winning proposal."

"Yes, Boss and Lawyer Jones want a meeting with the team as soon as possible."

"Then tell Peggy to schedule a meeting to coincide with my return next week."

Sheldon rested his hand on the phone in a long pause and absorbed what he had heard. Excavation in the North is huge, and competitors will look on with sore eyes.

CHAPTER NINE

Sheldon woke up the next day at eleven in the morning; the sun was beaming through the louvers; traffic was zipping along the highway, and the side streets below were lively with movements. He showered, dressed, and proceeded to the down elevators.

Mrs. Cicci was making her way back from the bakery, "Good Morning Mr. Morgan she said; Mr. Cicci was two steps behind her, trying to keep up; the concierge called out from his booth, "Going for breakfast, Mr. Morgan?"

"I'm not feeling hungry now, my friend; going for fresh air."

Sheldon felt like a leisurely walk would clear the cobwebs that had formed in his head. His walk led him through Marie Curtis Park to adjacent Lake Ontario beach. He stopped and stared at the lake. The water was calm and peaceful; boats sailed further out; people meandered; it had been a lovely day for a stroll. And as Sheldon walked along the shore, his feet left imprints in the wet sand. The pebbles he tossed into the lake bounced atop the water before they sunk. And he mused about his future and how he might remain relevant in the years ahead. Sadly, though, he might have to decide between living in Jamaica and living in Ontario. He was not ready to consider concrete domestic plans; he would commute to Etobicoke when needed and make his home in Montego Bay his permanent residence.

He might not have agonized anymore if there was nothing else to consider, but his late wife Blossom had bequeathed all of her assets to him, which made him wealthier than ever and vulnerable to women seeking rich men. So he opened his mouth and said to no one, "How does one remain humble with such a vast amount of wealth."

He twirled the band on his ring finger. Again, Sheldon felt uncomfortable; instead, he preferred to remain a simple man.

"Boss, you have given much and have much more to give; the big problem is you keep getting more all the time." Dixon was pragmatic; that was his analysis when he and Sheldon talked about simplicity.

Then Sheldon turned and walked the narrow winding path back into Marie Curtis Park. He noticed his favorite long bench underneath a big tree was unoccupied. He sat down with outstretched legs; his gaze was centered on the space in front of him. He was holding a dry bramble in his right hand. No amount of contemplation could satisfy his feelings at that moment. There were few people in the Park, which was what Sheldon preferred. A drizzle started. He contemplated returning home, but instead, he looked around for shelter. A woman walked by, pushing a cart with what looked like everything she owned, a man walked up to him and asked for spare change, and a young cyclist climbed the steps to the landing near the bus loop with his bicycle on his shoulder. Sheldon studied the wedding band on his finger, and its significance stirred him; he vowed to always keep his wife Blossom foremost in his thoughts.

Further out, he saw a woman sitting on a long bench reading loose pages. A large brown leather bag and an umbrella were on the seat next to her. He had seen her before, on the other days when he had come to Marie Curtis Park. The drizzle came down harder; Sheldon found a dry spot and sat. Suddenly he heard a woman's voice, "You're not wearing socks; your feet must be cold." The woman held out an unopened pair of dark gray socks. He recognized the large brown leather bag in the woman's hand, looked across to where a woman had always sat, and then looked closely at the woman in front of him. He realized she was the same person and did not consider accepting the socks prudent. But he did notice her crisp beige turtleneck sweater, sharp dark gray slacks, a dark gray toque that showed dangling earrings, and shiny black ankle boots; she might not have been a homeless person as Sheldon had been thinking. He furrowed his brow.

"You give away socks to people in Marie Curtis Park," he asked.

"Yes, people's feet get cold, especially in this weather. Please accept them."

And though Sheldon was hesitant at first, he relented and accepted the socks.

That day, Sheldon wore a pair of black Gucci leather loafers without socks and dark gray slacks. Black wool cardigan over a lavender shirt and black open-front, hip-length overcoat.

The woman noticed the pair of expensive loafers Sheldon had been wearing and wondered under what circumstances he came to have them. He might not have been homeless as she thought.

"I hope the socks will keep your toes warm...." She trailed off, but she wanted to say, *Who the hell are you, mister?*

Sheldon briefly considered the woman and concluded he had no desire to participate if her approach were a game; he was preoccupied and would ignore distractions.

The air under the woman's turtleneck sweater had gotten warm. She was concerned that she had infringed on the man's privacy. She thought it necessary to give more clarification.

"I give socks to people in the park, at train stations, at bus stops ... any place where I notice people not wearing socks, during wintry weather."

But, again, the attorney nature of the woman came into play; she attempted to make the case that she was an honest person wishing to do good.

"My name is Jolene Anderson," she said, mindful of her intrusion and acknowledging her tendency to get into scrapes was a weak point. Sheldon was unconcerned. She waved goodbye and climbed the steps out of the Park.

At four o'clock, Sheldon exited Marie Curtis Park. The evening sun was shining on his face; he held a hand over his forehead to shield his eyes from the glare. Residents were coming in from work; young mothers with their babies in strollers ventured out, and everyone was lively. Sam, the concierge, shuffled into his security booth to begin the night shift, and Mr. and Mrs. Cicci entered the lobby from their evening walk.

Later, when Sheldon checked his phone messages, he heard one from Father Templeton, inviting him for lunch at the Rectory the following day at one. He immediately returned Father Templeton's phone call. Father Templeton answered on the fifth ring. He sounded preoccupied.

"Hello, Sheldon," he said, "how are you, my son? I was in the backyard raking the leaves when the phone rang," he chuckled.

"I would be pleased to have lunch with you at the Rectory tomorrow at one."

"Very well, see you then."

Lunch with Father Templeton is timely; Sheldon had contemplated meeting with the Rector before returning to Montego Bay.

CHAPTER TEN

It poured buckets of rain the night before, and the fog that set in left the atmosphere dull. Sheldon phoned Mason.

"Mason, bring the Ferrari to the Rotunda, please." When Sheldon stepped outside the lobby, he suddenly noticed how green the grounds were. The fall chill had not yet penetrated the bright-colored flowers, and the red roses were still hardy.

Sheldon did not retain Mason's services; that day but chose to drive the Ferrari himself. Traffic was slow-moving; however, he arrived at the Rectory ln good time.

"Sheldon, my son, you look well." Father Templeton said when he greeted Sheldon at the Rectory door.

"Come in, sit down," Father Templeton pointed Sheldon to a cushioned side chair in the hall. Except for his slight paunch, Father Templeton looked strong. And the gray slacks and collarless white grandad shirt he was wearing showed him cool on a warm rainy day.

Father Templeton invited Sheldon to walk with him through his vegetable garden at the back of the Rectory. Everything looked fresh and green. The tomatoes, peppers, and green beans were ready for reaping.

"Homegrown vegetables taste so much better," Father Templeton said, absorbed in his vegetable garden. But Sheldon was itching to get the Rector's opinion on a pressing matter.

"Pardon me, Father Templeton," Sheldon said.

Father Templeton turned around. "Yes?"

"How soon is too quick to be intimate again after Blossom?"

Father Templeton raised an eyebrow.

"It is up to you, Sheldon—know that the days, weeks, months, and even years ahead might be lonely; take a break for as long as necessary; it comes down to you."

"It will not be as easy for me—I am not a young man, I am still attractive, and I am wealthy—I am in a quandary."

Father Templeton chuckled lightly.

"My son, you forgot to add; you are astute. In the past, you have made wise decisions under challenging circumstances, and for as long as I have known you, you have been accurate. I am confident you will make the right decision when the time comes.

You have my blessings."

The two men continue the conversation until Mrs. Templeton announces, "Lunch is on the table."

Over lunch, Father Templeton references the endowment Blossom's deceased husband, David Clark, had bequeathed his parish community. Father Templeton suggests his parish would graciously accept additional donations from Sheldon. "Gordon Rusk will see to it," Sheldon said.

Sheldon remembers the day when he met Father Templeton. He and Blossom had been dining out when Father Templeton and his wife entered the restaurant. Father Templeton had been a close friend of Blossom and David Clark. He understood the significance of cordial relationships, so when Blossom introduced Sheldon as her dear friend, Father Templeton said, *"Your dear friend is my dear friend Mrs. Clark …I'm pleased to meet you, Mr. Morgan."*

After lunch with Father Templeton, Sheldon accepted blessings and said goodbye to the Rector and his wife.

When Sheldon returned home from lunch with Father Templeton, he noticed Mrs. Cicci waiting with a covered dish in the lobby.

"Mr. Morgan, I made lasagna and a loaf of crusty bread and brought you some—Mrs. Morgan always liked my lasagna, too….."

Thank you, Mrs. Cicci." Sheldon accepted the meal from Mrs. Cicci and walked toward an open elevator; he entered his Suite within seconds.

Living in Suite 2108 and coping with the after-effects of Blossom's passing was overwhelming. Pieces of evidence of happy times with Blossom were glaring everywhere—her favorite paintings on the wall, the chair she sat on, her favorite perfumes on top of the dresser, and her closet with the outfits she wore were in place. Loose ends will take time to tie up.

Sheldon had decided to visit the Chalet for relaxation, as Gordon had suggested. The following day Mason would drive Sheldon to Collingwood. He picked up the phone. "Gordon, I go to the Chalet for four days starting tomorrow—you can reach me there if necessary."

"I am glad you decided to go; include a game or two of golf."

Mason stayed in Collingwood, too, to take care of Sheldon's point A to point B travels and be ready to do security guard duties.

George and Gaby Turner, owners of the variety store at the foot of the hill, were standing at the counter when Sheldon walked into the shop.

"Hello, Mr. Morgan," Gaby said. "We noticed the workers at the Chalet." George cut in.

"Renovations on the Chalet, and workers on the rest of the property, brought lots of business to our shop; thank you." George continued.

Sheldon walked the shop aisle, picked up things, and placed them in his handbasket. George approached. "Did you find everything, Sir?"

"I'm looking for triple-A batteries, George,"

Sheldon said. "Coming up, Mr. Morgan," George said.

While at the Chalet, Sheldon's work habits kicked in. He phoned Gordon Rusk.

"Gordon—I understand you've been busy all morning with phone calls."

"Right you are, Sheldon, and one of those calls was from your sister-in-law Odette Black."

"Why did Odette call you, Gordon?"

"Odette expressed surprise that Blossom left only a token amount of money for her in her Will. She had expected to receive the property in Jamaica, initially willed to Blossom by her father. She had hoped Blossom would bequeath that property to her—I explained the distinctions; I told her she was free to seek additional legal advice."

"But Gordon, it should be okay to let Odette have that property; I own it now; that is true; however, I should be able to gift it to her if I so desire."

"I don't see any reason you couldn't, Sheldon. I will look into the matter."

"Thanks, man. And Gordon, when you meet with Jerry Butler, my stockbroker, ask him to research the airline stock I talked with him about last Thursday. I want to buy the maximum shares possible in Caribbean Airways."

"Absolutely."

"I will phone you when I return to Etobicoke."

Sheldon considered Odette's desire to own her father's home. Then he remembered a conversation he had had with Blossom about the ownership of the property after the passing of her mother, Margareta.

Blossom had quoted her mother as saying, "*Your father was clear; he wanted you to have this property.*"

With Margareta now deceased and Odette living closer to the property, Sheldon felt it right to pass ownership to her; hopefully, Gordon would find a way to make it a reality.

PART TWO

HAPPENSTANCE!

She noticed his dark brown eyes. *Behold a gorgeous man,* she said to herself. The brother was tall, with broad shoulders, clean-shaven, with mahogany, flawless skin. He was the kind of man that turned a woman's head.

CHAPTER ELEVEN

A Criminal Prosecutor with pizazz

Jolene Georgina Moore, first of two daughters born to an immigrant family from Kingston, Jamaica, always remembers the two-bedroom bungalow she grew up in, situated on Bathurst Street in Toronto. She was born in Toronto, went to school in Toronto, and knew all about living there. Jolene studied hard and made good grades; she was the example her parents expected her sister Patricia Moore to follow. Her parents anticipated one or both of their daughters becoming lawyers or doctors. Jolene did not disappoint them. She delighted her father when she passed the bar examinations. "The Honda Prelude is our gift for such an outstanding achievement." Her father had said.

Adolphe Moore, generally known as Dolphie, Jolene's father, suffered an industrial accident, and even though he received enough compensation to start a grocery store business, the physical pain persisted. Jolene's mother, Mauve Moore, ran the grocery store business; before that, she had been a nurse at the city hospital. Patricia Moore operates her hair boutique adjoining her parents' grocery store.

Jolene is the daughter who confided in her mother on all matters; although she has not always heeded her mother's advice, she would, at least, consider them.

"But I want to be married and have five or six children." So she said to her mother.

"You better get cracking, honey," her mother had replied.

Jolene Moore was over thirty, gorgeous, with long dark brown twist curls and dark brown eyes, ready to be snatched up by a man willing to settle down. Her mother was correct; she should get cracking if she were serious about producing children. But, on the other hand, Jolene would not sidestep a promising legal career.

Before starting her new job in the prosecutor's office in Toronto, Jolene took a short vacation in Kingston, Jamaica. Her grandma Gladys from her father's side of the family still lived in a beautiful bungalow in the hills outside of Kingston, where Jolene stayed on visits.

On the day in question, Jolene scrutinized the lunch menu while sitting in the dining room at the Pegasus Hotel. The lunch was zesty, which made her hesitant. Then, suddenly, she heard a clear male voice.

She looked up. His gaze pulled at her.

"The sista is looking fine," he said.

He had noticed her beautiful hair, smooth bronze skin, and bare shoulders. Her manicured fingernails rested on the menu cover. He could tell she was not from the area.

She noticed dark brown eyes. *Behold a gorgeous man,* she said to herself. The brother was tall, had broad shoulders, was clean-shaven, and had mahogany brown skin. He was the kind of man that turned a woman's head. His skin tone showed he could have been living in cooler climes. He wore shorts that showed enough of him to presume; his shirt was unbuttoned, and his aviator sunglass hitched into his crew-neck undershirt.

She accepted his comment about *looking fine,* being familiar with the native jargon, and the tendencies of many Jamaicans to be up-front in their admiration of others.

"Have you made up your mind about your meal?" He continued.

"Not yet," she replied.

"The grilled fish with lemon butter sauce and green salad is delicious." The stranger said. Jolene thanked him for assisting her with choosing her meal.

"Care to sit with me on the Patio outside?"

"And you are?" Jolene trailed off, stunned by his boldness.

"Tyrone … Tyrone Anderson."

"Sure, Tyrone Anderson, I will sit with you outside on

the Patio."

When they settled at the table, Tyrone said.

"So—why were you sitting by yourself, Miss…." he trailed off.

Jolene hesitated. She understood his cultural audaciousness, but his curious pursuit of a deep conversation was intrusive. She looks at him with narrowed eyes.

He smiles, showing perfectly set teeth.

She relented, "My name is Jolene…Jolene Moore." They converse way into the afternoon. The two weeks of warm days and cool nights convinced Jolene and Tyrone they were meant for each other; they were confident that marriage was the next step.

When Jolene Moore married thirty-six-year-old Tyrone Anderson, she had been fresh out of law school; although Mauve Moore was thrilled to learn about Jolene's new love, she was amazed at the fast pace at which it was happening.

"Your relationship with Tyrone is moving rather quickly," Mauve said when Jolene announced her wedding day. Mauve knew her daughter had a habit of ending relationships when a wrinkle appeared, and she was terrified that Jolene and Tyrone's decision was too hasty. Moreover, Dolphie Moore was uneasy about the planned destination wedding in Ocho Rios and might easily have relinquished his role of walking his daughter down the aisles. Despite the family's misgivings, they joined in a beautiful wedding in a thatched house near the beach in Ocho Rios, Jamaica.

Four years later, two pregnancies occurred, which produced two boys and a marriage that had gone off the rails. Jolene's chronic fear of not sustaining a permanent relationship haunted her.

It was March 3, ten in the morning. Jolene's sons were with their father at Wendy's, having breakfast. Jolene's eyes were red from lack of sleep and wet with tears. Calico, her cat, jumped on the bathroom counter with a meow, sensing a need to comfort her mistress. Jolene patted the cat and let it down from the counter.

"Tyrone's shit is bothering me," she said to the cat, snot running down her nose.

That morning Jolene was on her way to an appointment with an attorney named Jose Montoy, a colleague of the courts and a person she had known for some time. The meeting with Montoy was not one she relished; nevertheless, she had intended to launch her private law career. Of all her colleagues and friends, Jose Montoy was the one lawyer willing to assist her aspirations.

Jolene picked up the phone on the nearby coffee table and dialed her mother as she often does when in distress. Mauve Moore recognized Jolene's call from the phone display; Mauve knew her daughter had been in a funk for a long while, and she would not let her daughter's calls go unanswered.

"Hello dear…how are you?"

"Hi, Mom…Why do you ask me the same

question—*how are you*—every time I call? I am fine, Mom, just fine."

At first, Jolene did not want to talk about her impending divorce with her parents; now, she had no choice; it was out in the open, and the whole thing depressed her. Her mother had become friends with Sheldon's mother, and they discussed the matter.

"Bring the boys over if you need a break," Mauve said, ignoring Jolene's sassy response.

"Mom... Tyrone is who I need a break from.... He's making things difficult for me ... but it makes no difference; I've made up my mind ...."

"I don't understand, Jo; what could be so complicated that the two of you cannot resolve?"

"Please, Mom, give it a rest, don't get emotionally involved in this... we're opposite ....our differences are stark. I'm leaving him." Jolene switched the phone to her other ear.

"Mom, are you still there?"

"Yes, honey; you and Tyrone are opposite? Like how?"

"Listen to this, Mom—like his newfound religion, like how the job at City Hall did not work out, and he sits in front of the TV every moment he gets and watches church TV, like how he wants to drag me to his church every Sunday...I am a prosecutor Mom; I put guilty people behind bars—Tyrone should find a job—he is stifling me."

"You got to be out of your mind—breaking up your marriage over that..." her mother trailed off indignantly. Mauve paused long enough for Jolene to ask, "Mom, are you still there?"

"Yes, dear, I am just worried about my grandsons," Mauve continued.

Jolene became silent at the other end of the phone; she wanted to say aloud to her mother; *Mom, those are not the real reasons Tyrone and I are divorcing.*

Then Jolene said, "Look, Mom---those unpleasant habits of Tyrone irk me."

Her mother sighed. "I talked with Yvonne last week. She is longing to see you. Did you tell Yvonne that you're considering a divorce?" Mauve pretended she had not been talking with Yvonne, Tyrone's mother.

"Not *considering a divorce,* Mom…separated and filed for a divorce…his mother already knows."

"You are separated and living in the same house?" Mauve asked.

"Stranger things have happened, Mom."

"Fine, it's up to you and Tyrone." Mauve shoved her two hands into her deep apron pockets, "I am sad about this."

"I'm coming to see you, Mom—need a bottle of guava jelly and green bananas; see you soon."

The truth was Jolene felt guilty that she might have torn apart her family because of her hurry to get ahead with her career. She had sleepless nights thinking about how unfortunate she had been to be solely responsible for the enormous monthly rent for her family's exclusive condominium and the monthly lease on her Mercedes Benz. Her in-laws made no secret that their son had rushed into a quick glamorous marriage with her, and though she was an attorney, they still felt their son should have married further up.

Mauve Moore was looking forward to seeing Jolene; she had not seen her for several months. Then, at the sound of the creek in the shop door, Mauve turned her head and saw Jolene entering. She was surprised at how worn Jolene had been. Then, after a warm embrace, Mauve said.

"Jojo, you want some lunch?" Mauve looked closer at Jolene.

"You are thin, Jo. Have you not been eating?"

"Not much, Mom—I have no appetite."

"Honey, do not let your father see you thin like this; he'll start fretting."

"How can I eat, Mon, when I'm such a bad mother and an incompetent wife; Mom, I consented for Tyrone to keep my boys."

Tears welled up in Jolene's eyes.

Mauve pulled her daughter to her chest.

"Hush, honey, you are a mother; you love your boys; they will come to you in time."

Mauve's imagination was rich; her feelings about what had been going on with Jolene and Tyrone were that there must be underlying matters that came to the surface; Dolphie never doubted Mauve's discernment. So when she said, "Dolphie, I can't help wondering if there was something deeper going on with those two." Dolphie remained silent and let Mauve's imagination run wild.

CHAPTER TWELVE

It was not Jolene Anderson's intention. It happened extremely fast. Jolene married, carried two boys, and became disheartened within four years.

In the beginning, the possibilities for Jolene and Tyrone seemed endless. They had mapped out a future that ensured their success, except that the arrival of their first child, followed by a second child soon after, derailed their plans. But Jolene would not be put off by any obstacle; she advanced the family outlook with full support for Tyrone's political ambitions. The stress of work, the worry of young parenthood, and their financial frailty began to show in their marriage. A stress break became necessary.

It did not matter Jolene's divorce became her parents' dinner table talk. It didn't count her marital situation widened the chasm between her and her mother-in-law. She didn't even care; her mother-in-law no longer spoke to her; Jolene had done what she thought was right.

Tyrone loved being a father to his boys, but that did not make Jolene feel better. Her struggle to provide for the family was more than she could endure. Moreover, having to secure loans from Jose Montoy, as embarrassing as it had been, was not as awful as going to Tyrone's parents with hat-in-hand, even though they would not refuse to assist their son and grandsons.

Jolene was desperate enough to disclose her predicament about her husband's unemployed status and her family's financial miseries to Jose Montoy; of course, she had to confide in someone other than her mother, or Tyrone's mother, for that matter. Things had been rocky, with her trying to make the best of her job as a prosecutor and Tyrone himself trying to find work between looking after the boys while she worked late at the office.

Jolene was surprised at how quickly Montoy had made funds available when she requested. And even as she showed a positive front, she could not push past the shame of seeking Jose Montoy's financial help; in the end, Jolene and Tyrone lost their fight to save their marriage.

Jolene met Jose Montoy, the defense attorney representing a tainted property developer named James Lloyd Green, in the lunch queue at the Magistrate's cafeteria. So she was intrigued when Jose offered to pick up the tab at the cashier's counter. They made acquaintance later, and she found out he and she had been in law school around the same, but somehow, she had escaped his sight, and now she was recovering from a messy divorce.

Jose appeared in Jolene's courtroom more than once, and she had said hello to him often enough during lunch in the Cafeteria. Then, she confessed her financial troubles during a terrible, stressful period. He offered her loans to subsidize rent and other necessities, which she accepted, but she had since recovered, to some extent, and was now interested in obtaining a business reference. In addition, Jolene recognized Montoy's steady career advancement and considered collaborating on legal matters a good move.

Jose Montoy stood five feet seven inches in platform shoes. A man of medium build, graying at the temples, 55 years old, graduated from Law School in Toronto seven years earlier. He first articled at a small firm in Toronto; then, he held down a three-year stint in a mid-sized firm west of Toronto as a partner. He sees his legal wins as feathers in his periwig.

He wore expensive suits and sported a costly wristwatch. A native of The Philippines, Montoy had no qualms about his impoverished beginnings, but he never wanted to return to those days. Instead, he was determined to be the first of his parents' eight children to go to College and exit with a degree, and he had intended to return to his homeland to practice law, notwithstanding he later changed his mind.

Monday afternoon, 2 o'clock. Jolene was

waiting in the reception area of Johnson and Golding Law Offices to see Montoy. She looked around—cushioned sofa, two matching chairs, L-shaped Cherrywood reception desk with matching four-drawer credenza, water cooler strategically placed beside a huge rubber plant, soft rock music coming through a built-in stereo system. It seemed like a nice place to work. Jolene was amazed at how Jose held down good positions in law firms. The sign on the receptionist's desk read *Christina Redpath*.

"Jolene?" asked a silver-haired woman looking at her over wire-rim glasses.

"Yes, Ma'am," Jolene answered,

"Mr. Montoy will see you now."

Jolene glanced at her reflection in a mirrored side panel on the front door. She shook her head from side to side to be sure her curs hung right, smoothed out the legs of her pantsuit with both hands, and adjusted her pea-shaped pearl earrings. She walked alongside Miss Redpath down a short hall. Miss Redpath knocked and opened Jose's office door.

"Thank you, Miss Redpath."

"Hello, Jose."

"Hello, Jolene."

"Thanks for seeing me at such short notice. "

"Not at all, Jolene," Montoy pointed her to the cushioned client's chair by the side of his big desk. He curled his right palm under his chin, propped up by his elbow, on top of his desk. "What brings you here today, Jolene?"

Jolene pulled her chair to the edge of Jose Montoy's desk

"I was talking with myself recently, and I conclude, as a criminal defense attorney, I could negotiate less harsh sentences for the accused, offer vigorous defense to people who need it, and…" she paused to sip from the coffee Christina Redpath had given her. She could tell it came out of a coffee machine, and coffee from coffee machines tasted unpleasant, but she took another sip. Jose Montoy stroked his chin, "I see."

" ….and the compensation is substantial." Jolene went on.

Montoy arched his brow to imply that what Jolene had said was not a good enough reason to launch a private law career. Then he said, with a chuckle, *"Bulshit."*

Jolene looked at Jose Montoy with narrowed eyes; she never thought using a metaphor like *bullshit* was becoming anyone. Still, Jolene was ready to consider Montoy's reasoning.

Then Montoy said, "I had hoped you would be in the prosecutor's role at the trial of James Green." Jolene clenched her fists in her lap. She would love to put James Green behind bars for his misdemeanors.

In more than one of Jose Montoy's criminal cases, Jolene had been the prosecutor; suddenly, she became uncomfortable. She was on the verge of making a statement; instead, Jolene pivoted, "Jose, this career move is what I wanted all along."

Jose remained silent for a long moment, "Sometimes, the most successful thing a person has done began with a leap into the unknown. I'll do all I can for you," Montoy sounded sincere.

The intercom on Montoy's desk announced his next client. He rose from his chair, and Jolene did the same. Jolene entered a down elevator.

The following morning, she lay in her tiny attic room, thinking how arrogant she had been during her meeting with Jose Montoy. Finally, she admitted that humility would be necessary if she wished to go forward. After all, Jose was kind enough to assist her financially when she needed help, and even though she was not pleased with her performance the previous day, she knew Jose would not break his promise to help her in every way he could.

It was, by then, 10 in the morning. Jolene picked up her phone on the night table and dialed.

Miss Redpath put the call through to Jose.

Hello Jolene, good to hear from you."

"Jose, I want to say thanks for all the help you gave me."

"Not at all, Jolene; what's up?"

"This attic apartment on the east side where I have lived since my divorce is driving me crazy. I am unhappy—and though the rent is inexpensive and the place is accessible to the city, I am looking for a better place."

"Don't worry, I'll keep my ear to the ground and let you know when I hear about a nice place," Jose said. Jolene felt relieved.

Then a short time later, when she had just reached her apartment after a long day and dropped her brown briefcase on the futon in the corner, the phone rang.

"Hi, Jolene, Jose here. Pack your things; I will take you to better living quarters."

"You found better living quarters for me?" Jolene was excited.

"I prepared a beautiful room in my home for you, Jolene. You will love it. I will be at your place in an hour to help you pack—also, I am starting work with Gordon Rusk, CEO of the famous Gordon Rusk Law Firm, in a month."

"That's wonderful. Jose."

"And I got work for you in Gordon Rusk Law Firm." "I am with you, Jose."

Jolene moved into Jose Montoy's beautiful home in North York, just outside Toronto. Not long after, she became aware of his fascination for living with more than one woman under his roof. He set up extreme rules for living with him, and for a long time, Montoy resided with more than one woman in a consensual relationship. He would not readily admit it, but his arrangement with the women in his household was polygamous. Finally, however, Montoy's new addition, Jolene Anderson, agreed to his rules for living with him.

Montoy's harem was a sore spot for Jolene, for though she wanted to be with him in a loving relationship, she was not happy to share him with two other women. And Jose would not commit to changing his lifestyle; he insisted he could provide for and serve all three women.

The phone rang, and the call displayed her mother's name. "Hello, Mom"

"How are you keeping, Jojo," her mother asked.

"I am well, Mom; how are you and daddy?"

"We are well. We invite you and your sister, Pauline, over for Sunday dinner." Jolene paused. She remembers her mother's reaction when she told her about the living arrangement with Jose Montoy. The conversation was stressful, *"You agreed to your man laying with another woman under the same roof?"*

"Jose and I are in love, and I agree with the arrangement—I have no doubt he can care for three women, sexually and financially."

"But, Jo, listen to your mother; leave the polygamist before something terrible happens."

"Jose Montoy is going in the right direction; Mom, it might be an excellent move to settle down with him for a while."

"Settled down? No one settles you down with a polygamist, my dear."

"It's not like that, Mom."

"Be careful, Jojo, don't get hurt."

Dinner with her parents and sister was an occasion for another family meeting, and the discussions were often about Jolene's relationship challenges. Jolene switched the phone to her other ear.

"Sorry, Mom, I can't come to dinner; I must read up on cases."

Mauve Moore expressed her disappointment that Jolene could not come to dinner. They said goodbye and hung up.

Despite Montoy's controlling nature and Mauve Moore's warning that Jolene should be careful, she decides to remain in Montoy's home.

The following day was a typical fall day—the outdoor chill required a warm sweater, the breeze tossed colorful leaves around and about, and people walked along the sidewalk with zest. Jolene lingered on the pavement and inhaled clean, crisp air, thankful that Montoy had followed through on his promise of legal work alongside him in the prestigious law firm of Gordon Rusk.

That day, Jolene went to Marie Curtis Park to read up on pending cases. The quiet of the Park is why she regularly visits, and she brought with her a stack of pages to go through and make notes. Close to the steps leading out of the park to the train station is where Jolene sat. She threw a thick blanket over a long bench and lay back.

Jolene noticed a man sitting crossed-legged on a long bench near where she was; she had seen him at the same spot once or twice before, and she thought it strange that his feet were sockless on a cold day. Her first instinct was to ignore her eyesight. But instead, she walked over and handed him the pair of gray socks she had purchased for her ex-husband's birthday gift. And though the man appeared homeless, Jolene was surprised by his expensive attire, which made her apologize for the intrusion. Furthermore, Jolene was taken aback by how unappreciative the man was, assuming he could not afford a pair of socks to warm his toes. Finally, a drizzle started; Jolene opened her umbrella and exited the Park.

CHAPTER THIRTEEN

"When do you plan to move out, Son?"

"Dad, you know I hate plans."

Thirty-six-year-old Tyrone Anderson told his parents, Ezra and Yvonne Anderson that he would move into his own place when he found the right woman to marry. So when he met and married the beautiful young prosecutor Jolene Moore, he knew the time had come to move to a place of his own.

All along, Tyrone had lived privileged, mindful of his status as his parents' only offspring; he took advantage of their love and adoration and the spending money they doled out.

It had been a time of political upheaval in Tyrone's homeland, Jamaica. And although he was a boy of thirteen years at that time, he was aware of the viciousness of the situation.

"The political heat is too much, Ezra—we should consider immigrating to Canada—our chance for better living." So said Yvonne Anderson in a moment of fear.

Ezra and Yvonne were worried that Tyrone would witness out-of-control crime and violence in the streets of Kingston. So the family uprooted to Ontario at the invitation of Yvonne's best friend, the bestselling author.

The Andersons had been members of the upper class in their home country. So when Ezra Anderson, a professor of Psychology at the University, and Yvonne, a municipal politician, decided to move away from Jamaica, they were surprised to discover that Jamaica's affluence was much different from the affluence in their new country, Canada.

Eventually, Ezra's professor education landed him a job in the public school system in Toronto; however, Yvonne's Jamaican politics was unrelated. Nonetheless, Tyrone's upbringing and schooling in Toronto served him well.

Upon graduation from university with a degree in Political Science, Tyrone's parents gifted him a holiday to Jamaica. He had been at the Pegasus Hotel and had made his way to the dining room for lunch when he noticed an attractive woman sitting by herself and thumbing through the Menu. He saw her frustration and offered to help her decide on a meal.

Yvonne Anderson, the beloved mother of Tyrone, remembered the day her son called from Kingston, Jamaica, to announce he was in love.

"Mom, I found the girl I'd been looking for."

"Boy,"...his mother said, loud enough for his father to hear her, "pack your bags and come home this minute before you make a mistake."

Suzie's Coffee Bar in downtown Toronto, where Tyrone sat with his mother over coffee, was lively with late-evening coffee patrons.

"Mom," he said, tracing the rim of his cup. "Jolene and I are meeting for a quick bite at Sheriff today—we're cool with the divorce—we made the right decision concerning our boys."

"I've never heard such a thing—how can you be cool with having your sons grow up without their parents living together? In my book, this is not cool." Yvonne was indignant.

"Mom, I know what you are thinking—I'll say it for you, *Son; I told you so.*"

"Son, this is not a celebration," Yvonne said, peering into her coffee cup. I am sorry it came to this—I am genuinely sorry."

Yvonne felt an amount of guilt. She never accepted Jolene with open arms, and Jolene knew it. And though Jolene's mother tried to bring the two families together, Dolphie convinced himself that Ezra was much too self-important to be a relatable addition to the family. Yvonne inhaled a deep breath.

"Coffee is bitter," Yvonne said, slurping on the last drop.

"Can't be that bitter, Mom; you drank all of it. Want a refill?" Tyrone asked. He watched his mother pull the swig louder on the droplets of coffee.

"No, son, I am thinking ... thinking a lot."

"About what, Mom," Tyrone asked, though he would rather not know; he beckoned the server; she brought a fresh pot of coffee.

"The amount of money your father and I spent on your destination wedding in Ocho Rios... your father's exotic outfits were too expensive, and oh, his insistence on first-class travel ... that was a waste of hard-earned money." She frowned; the lines around her chin deepened. "Nevertheless, we did all we could to show you we were proud."

"Mom, please don't blame me; I'd much rather have gone to City Hall here in Toronto and married Jolene."

You went and joined religion—that was not in the cards for Jolene. The boys didn't ask for this; in a few years, you and Jolene have to explain why their mommy and daddy aren't living together."

"Mom, things will work out just fine."

"You think I don't see—your hair is receding—stress, I say; pure stress."

"I was in love with Jolene, Mom—I probably still am," Tyrone smiled.

"That is well and good, but you always break your rules about falling in love when you meet a beautiful woman ... get over your mistake, son!"

Yvonne was right. Tyrone was missing Jolene, and he was stressed. "Come home, my son, and bring my grand-babies." Yvonne's eyes welled up.

Tyrone had been in the process of re-thinking his desire to work in the Ontario Public Sector. He thought public service employment might be a good jump-off point to his goal of entering Ontario Politics. Still, he realizes there were no shortcuts to his ambition as an Ontario politician.

In a joint arrangement, he had parted ways with Jolene. Now Jolene wants to cut loose entirely.

Honestly, I never imagined it would come to this; our relationship seemed fitting. How could something that seemed so right have been wrong? Now I am a single parent with two sons. Tyrone said to himself and sighed.

He stroked his cheeks; a layer of hair was forming; he had not been paying close attention to how he looked lately.

The temperature in Suzie's Coffee Bar had risen as more coffee drinkers came in. Tyrone held back from asking his mother if she was ready to leave.

"You are forming hair growth on your face?" Yvonne was still talking.

"You ought not to be careless about grooming. Now more than ever is the time to be aware of how you look," Yvonne went on.

Tyrone eyed his mother; he wanted to ask her if everything were okay, but he knew she would change the subject to talking about him and his problems with Jolene. These are the times he wished he had siblings.

"Mom, it is time you change your focus on me ... I am a grown man; I can take care of the unpleasantness of life."

"I shouldn't judge you, son."

Tyrone had arranged a meeting with Jolene to talk about the next steps concerning the boys.

"Let us meet at Shariff for a drink and talk."

"About the boys?"

"Yes."

On seeing Jolene entering Shariff, Tyrone sat on a high stool at the window, looking out on passing vehicles. She joined him.

Jolene noticed Yvonne sitting off to the side; she was surprised that Tyrone allowed his mother to come along; she was an interloper, always sticking her nose into their business. Yvonne looked at Jolene with squinted eyes.

"I wish you had brought our sons with you."

"They were still in school when I left home, and Dad will pick them up."

Tyrone looked lean and exhausted. He often said he was the better parent, and Jolene had not been a good mother to the boys because of the long hours she had spent away from them, pouring over court documents; he was always the available parent. Still, just because she took the occurring family situation in strides did not mean she was not distraught.

Tyrone became introspective: "I admit my share of the blame for our marriage break up; still, I believe we allowed our parents to meddle in our affairs, and look where it got us."

Jolene agreed; her father, Dolphie Moore, was always wary of Tyrone's parents. He thought Ezra and Yvonne were braggadocious people, so much so Mauve Moore's disdain manifested at Jolene's wedding reception in Ocho Rios when, in Yvonne's hearing, Mauve said.

"Why, on earth, is Ezra's speech so long?"

Yvonne was deeply offended, and she said.

"Ezra will not have another opportunity such as this; Tyrone is our only offspring,"

The situation had put Dolphie on edge and might have caused an all-out brawl that could have been Mauve's fault, and Yvonne never forgave Mauve for almost ruining Tyrone's wedding reception.

In Shariff's, Jolene mentioned to Tyrone that she saw no future in the public prosecution's office, and possibilities in a large Toronto firm were more likely. She advised Tyrone that her colleague Jose Montoy had brought her to a large firm that recently hired him, and she was grateful for that.

"Is that your way of telling me you are dating so soon after our break-up?" Jolene ignored the question. Tyrone continued, "The boys and I will be settled in my parents' place."

"That is good; do my sons miss me."

"Yes."

"Will you let them see me when they want to?"

"Yes"

Tyrone looked at his wrist. "Sorry, I've got to go now. Good luck."

Jolene's eyes met Yvonne as she walked with Tyrone out of Suzie's Coffee Bar. She knew Yvonne blamed her for the break-up. Both Yvonne and Ezra never thought Jolene was right for their son. At that moment, Jolene felt abandoned. She looked around the room; there were chatter and laughter, and everyone seemed happy except her.

She picked up her purse and exited.

PART THREE

AND THEN IT HAPPENED

She noticed him smiling, likely remembering a precious moment; Jolene could not hold back her feelings any longer; she picked up her camera, tip-toed onto the verandah, and clicked three times in a row. The first click startled Sheldon; he did not see it coming; the second click caught him wide-eyed in horror, and he showed a polite smile on the third click. The moment left him stunned. Sheldon did not know what to make of it.

CHAPTER FOURTEEN

Montego Bay, Jamaica

It was Saturday morning of the long Easter weekend. Sheldon was walking to the pet store to purchase bird seeds. The morning was already warm for a March day. He heard the sound of vehicles and stepped on the sidewalk to give way. Dixon pulled up alongside him.

"What in God's name are you doing out so early, Dixon?"
"Going to the pet store. May I give you a lift?"
"How convenient, Dixon." Both men laugh.

After purchasing at the pet store, Sheldon and Dixon detoured to the North Site. Work had started two weeks before, and Dixon had hired three additional equipment operators. In addition, Sheldon was negotiating with Doug Williams to utilize Williams Construction Company's unused equipment.

"My company lost out on the North Site contract" Doug was furious though he agreed to Sheldon utilizing his unused equipment for a reasonable fee.

"Be sensible, Doug. Maybe it's your shitty work ethic catching up with you. Figure out what you want to do with your company; in the meantime, I am moving ahead with renting your equipment that sits idly in your yard."

"I can see it now, Boss; Mr. Doug is mentally exhausted, but he shouldn't blame other people; he has to keep on moving, revitalize his company and come back stronger," Dixon said.

"I hope he does, Dixon."

Operations had closed down that weekend for repairs to equipment at the West Hill mechanic shop. Sheldon had gone to West Hill to observe the men at work.

"Boss, you are checking on the guys," Dixon asked Sheldon.

"Not checking, hanging out with them,"

Sheldon leaned on the side of his truck, beaming with pride at the extent of his business. He reached into the back of his vehicle for bottled water to hand out. "Tell the guys to meet me at Cool

Runnings for lunch in an hour," he instructed Dixon.

Lunch hour at Cool Runnings was busy, with most pick-up orders.

"How goes the battle, *Sexy*?"

"I fight on; may I take your order, Sir?"

"Seven lunches; and beers as required."

" Very well, Mr. Sheldon."

Jerk chicken wings washed down with beer were just what the men wanted; each enjoyed a tasty lunch. Sheldon and Dixon stayed back for a short discussion.

The rainy Easter weekend closed out with the sun shining against the blue sky; fresh air flowed in abundance.

Excavation had stopped a week before the long weekend because of soggy ground and water-filled dug-out holes.

Sheldon went to his corporate office at 3 to meet with municipal council representatives regarding zoning restrictions and additional parking spaces.

Sheldon pushed back in his chair; and waited for a scheduled call from Gordon Rusk in Toronto. He sips the brew that Peggy placed on his desk.

"Hello, Gordon," Sheldon said when the phone on his desk rang, "sorry I missed your call earlier; I was out in the mud rearranging backhoes."

Hello, my friend; how's the weather down there?"

"It's a bright sun-shiny day—as they say—

come on down for a holiday."

"I would love to, pal, but no-can-do right now; got work to do for you."

"I say, take some time off."

"Sure—but first things first."

"What's up."

"Remember David Clark's daughter, Camile?"

"Yes, yes, I remember her. Last time I saw her was at Blossom's interment."

"I received word from a top-notch law firm that she's contesting Blossom's Will."

"Why the hell would she do that? Bloss didn't see it fit to will anything to her."

"She wants to claim Building Two of the Emerald Towers in Etobicoke."

"She What?" Sheldon took a drink from his coffee mug on his desk and crossed his long legs atop his polished desk.

"It could be costly and time-consuming on her part, though that would not be a problem for her; she can afford it. But, in any event, I don't think she has a leg to stand on."

"How so?

"According to estate laws here, Camile Clark is a self-supporting married adult; she has no claim of any kind upon any moral ground."

Sheldon stretched the length of his body in his chair and leaned back to make himself more comfortable.

Gordon continued. "Camile would like to see you disinherited; she believes it was not evident in her father's Last Will that Building Two of the Emerald Towers was solely bequeathed to Blossom to dispose of as she pleased. Under those circumstances, she believed she should be the rightful beneficiary of Building Two, based on her father's Will. When I prepared Mr. Clark's Last Will, I carefully considered the family situation regarding the distribution of Mr. Clark's properties. Mr. Clark was clear in the bequest of his legacy to Blossom. Therefore, your deceased wife Blossom Morgan's will to you of Building Two, Emerald Towers in Etobicoke stays. I will make the legal arguments on your behalf—you do not have to appear, but you do have to come to my 70th birthday dinner party in November," Gordon Rusk chuckled lightly.

"And, Sheldon, before I sign off, I must remind you that you casually mentioned you would bid for Ethica Mature Lifestyles a year ago. I heard through the grapevine that it might go up for sale. I researched the place; it needs renovation, and the owner is not prepared to spend monies on upgrades; he plans to retire and return to England permanently. Nevertheless, as you mentioned, it is an excellent investment at a perfect location for renaming Blosseque. So here's your chance to make another significant investment. I will delve more into the sale on your behalf and get details about it."

"Do I have to be over there for this?"

"Probably not, but we could close the deal when you come for my birthday party." Sheldon rose from his chair with the phone to his ear.

"You don't give a man time to prepare,"…he trailed off.

"A man like you needs little time to prepare—talk again soon, my friend."

Sheldon concluded a successful day at the office and a peaceful drive home.

He glanced around and saw that Caroline had gone to her quarters for the day, and Jimmy, the grounds man, was raking the leaves. Just then, Sheldon heard a knock at the front door.

"Come in, Dixon."

"Good evening, Boss; Mr. Barclay from West Hill site is with me; he brought you young coconut water for drinking."

"Hey Barclay, come in; thanks for the young coconut water."

"I know you enjoy the drink, Sir." The three men lounged on the Patio and chatted. Afterward, Dixon and Barclay left. Sheldon stayed on the Patio and watched the clouds crisscrossing the full moon.

CHAPTER FIFTEEN

The Emerald Towers, Tower Two, Etobicoke, Ontario

Sheldon Morgan arrived in Etobicoke in mid-October, just in time to see the spectacle of Autumn leaves turning red, yellow, and brown. He approached the lobby of Tower Two as a gust of wind sent dry leaves that the leaf rakers had banked against the curb, swirling and fluttering in the air.

He paused at the security desk to leave a message for his chauffeur Mason to be waiting in Tower Two's Rotunda to take him to Collingwood the following morning. Gordon Rusk had reported full completion of the renovation of the Chalet into a hotel and convention center.

"Welcome back, Mr. Morgan," Sam, the Concierge, said. Sheldon was happy to return to Suite 2108 though he had planned to stay at the Chalet for a week's rest; he would integrate Gordon Rusk's 70th birthday party.

In a phone call before Sheldon left Montego Bay, he had reminded Gordon of his plan to pick up the tab for his birthday party.

"You cannot do that, Sheldon."

"I can do as I please, Gordon, and I am pleased to tell you that you do as I say." Gordon knew better than to defy Sheldon.

The following morning, Mason was waiting in the Rotunda in his usual posture at the passenger side door of the Ferrari.

"I got coffee for you, Sir."

"Thank you, Mason."

The drive to Collingwood was relaxing.

After a restful afternoon, Sheldon visited George and his wife Gaby, the grocery store owners; then, he took a leisurely walk through the trees at the bottom of the hill. He later reclined on the Chalet's verandah.

He considered hiring a competent individual to see to the overall management of the Chalet property; a ski instructor would be an additional staff during winter; he would rely on Gordon Rusk to recruit qualified persons.

Gordon's birthday party was coordinated by *Cotton House*, a premier Events Planning Company. Special invitations were sent out well in advance to Gordon's close friends and associates.

On the evening of the event, Limousines lined

the Chalet entrance, and guests stepped out in fine apparel. Jose Montoy and Jolene Anderson, two recent additions to Gordon Rusk Law Firm, were on the guest list. The formality of the affair was remarkable—gentlemen dressed in Tuxedos, ladies in evening dresses. Jolene Anderson wore a black, long-sleeve cocktail dress designed with fine georgette material. The skirt was slightly above the knee with frills around the hem; a plunging Vee neckline completed the outfit. Jolene's hair was upswept; she wore black suede leather slingback shoes.

The convention hall at the Chalet, with colorful balloons and low-hanging streamers, the dining tables covered with white tablecloths, and an oversized chandelier hanging from the ceiling, illuminated the elegant room.

Soft music came from the live band on the other side of the lacquered floor; the DJ was fantastic.

Servers floated around with trays of appetizers; Champagne flutes clinked, and cutlery touched the edges of China gracefully. Guests were cheerful and chatty. The occasion was befitting the birthday of a principled attorney named Gordon Rusk.

Sheldon was seated at the head table, engrossed in conversation with Gordon. His noticeable presence in the dining room caught the gusts' attention. Husbands followed the wandering eyes of their wives but stayed silent. Sheldon's left hand occasionally rose to his chin, revealing Cartier Tortue's watch and gold cufflinks.

The Band struck up the Happy Birthday song, and everyone sang along to the delight of Gordon, who had been holding a champagne flute. He raised his flute high.

"Gordon is about to speak," someone said audibly.

Gordon cleared his throat, but instead of giving a speech, he said, "Let's Party."

The crowd erupted with delightful laughter, then came the song *Celebration Time,* and guests hit the dance floor.

Sheldon and Gordon continued chatting; humor went back and forth between them; the two men were comfortable with each other; then, Sheldon raised his flute and proposed a toast.

"Here's to many more happy birthdays to you, Gordon." Sheldon clinked his flute of champaign to Gordon's flute. Suddenly Clayton and Audrey Samuel, senior partners in Clayton's father's Law Firm, appeared. They both yelled Happy Birthday to Gordon, unconcerned about the party din.

The server poured more champagne into the champagne flutes. An extraordinary amount of laughter and affection flowed between everyone.

After a while, Sheldon and Gordon moved to the bar counter, still chatting and laughing with ease.

Slow waltz played, one after another; Jose Montoy approached Jolene to dance. At first, she squirmed. Jose Montoy took that to mean Jolene was not pleased with his behavior the night before when he asked permission to bed with him, and she had refused.

"Please forgive me," Jose Montoy said in a whisper. Then, finally, Jolene surrendered and slid into his arms; they danced to several slow songs.

Jose noticed Gordon and Sheldon in a discussion with Clayton and Audrey.

He slowly released Jolene's locked arm around his neck and joined them.

Sheldon and Gordon pretended not to notice Jose Montoy entering their presence.

Jose cleared his throat. "Happy Birthday Mr. Rusk; welcome back, Mr. Morgan."

Both men nodded.

Hello Mr. and Mrs. Samuel," Jose continued.

Jolene was itching to be by Jose's side. So she turned to the friend next to her and said, "Barbara, I will be back shortly."

Jolene dashed into the powder room to refresh her makeup, tuck in loose curls and make sure the Vee at the neck of her dress was set precisely in her bosom. Then she worked her way through the party crowd to the spot where Jose Montoy, Mr. Rusk, and Sheldon were standing. She approached and looped her arm into Jose's elbow. He turned and looked at Jolene with raised eyebrows.

"Happy birthday Mr. Rusk." Jolene smiled at Gordon Rusk.

Thank you, Mrs. Anderson."

Jolene found the term *Mrs. Anderson* inconvenient at that moment. She was not sure what her next move should be. She stretched her right hand to Sheldon, "Hello, Mr. Morgan, my name is Jolene Anderson." Sheldon shook her hand and smiled.

Jolene smiled back. Neither indicates they remember the other from the day in Marie Curtis Park.

"Mr. Rusk," Jolene's eyes were on Gordon, "Judge Marcus sent his regrets; the message was recorded on my phone just before I left the office this afternoon."

"He did reach me directly the day before…he would have loved to be here, but his granddaughter's graduation from high school is also today.

Jolene looked at Sheldon, "And Mr. Morgan, I hope you get an opportunity to see the Town of Collingwood; the sight is gorgeous this time of year."

"I'll try. Thank you." Sheldon recognized Jolene's charm.

Gordon waived the server over; everyone took a new flute of champaign. Jolene retreated into the packed dance crowd and found her way to her table.

Clayton guided Audrey onto the dance floor for a slow dance, and Gordon conversed with Sheldon and Jose at the bar counter.

After a while, the birthday party crowd fanned out. And guests retired to their reserved suites.

Jose Montoy approached Jolene at the door of her suite, and a disagreement arose. He was angry that she tried to wave him off earlier when he asked her to dance; furthermore, she had refused to have him in her bed the night before; as she was not interested in accommodating him.

"Jose, I refuse to have you in my bed; go to one of your other two mistresses," Jolene had said to Jose, and he was indignant.

"Well then, can I stay with you tonight?"

"That is not possible; I cannot risk anyone seeing you coming in or going out of my suite."

Jose pulled Jolene close and kissed her roughly, "How dare you send me away empty-handed?"

"You disgust me," Jolene said, turning her back to Jose. Then, Jose walked away, sorely disappointed.

Gordon Rusk bunked with Sheldon after his birthday party.

Eight the following morning, Gordon and Sheldon went to eat breakfast in the Chalet dining room. When they were seated, Gordon slid single pages over to Sheldon and said, "Take a look at these; no need to read them over; they are paid invoices for renovation work done on the Chalet project."

"Thanks, Gordon; I think you know what to do with them."

"Yes. I'll send these Invoices to Comptroller Aubrey Smith at Flanigan and Smith."

After that, they hit the highway in Gordon's car; commuters had just begun to veer onto the road.

Gordon put the car on cruise control; Sheldon's thoughts turned to Jose Montoy.

"Montoy exhibited an amount of loyalty to the Firm when he spoke with us last night."

"He is the same in court before a Judge."

"Does he own a home?"

"A huge home in North York."

"What about family?"

"He's not married; I know that—why all the questions?"

I am trying to form an opinion of him—I hope he will be a great asset to the Firm."

"Possibly—before long, young lawyers like Montoy branch out independently."

Gordon turned onto the access ramp to Etobicoke, rolled his car into the Rotunda of Building Two, and let Sheldon out from the passenger side.

CHAPTER SIXTEEN

With the expansion of the Chalet into a convention complex, it was time to hire an in-house property manager to replace the property management company. So when Gordon Rusk asked Jolene Anderson, criminal defense attorney and so-called pinch-hitter in his Law firm, to be the interim in-house property manager, she was delighted to oblige. But she would not have been as thrilled to accept the assignment had she not been anxious to be far away from Jose Montoy, her annoying suitor.

She knew the Chalet was renovated into a 30-room lodging and convention concept on one hundred acres of lush green space, with a golf course and a ski hill. And the chalet had been the winter home of wealthy Jamaican Sheldon Morgan and his deceased wife, Blossom Black.

"I would be pleased to fill in until you find someone suitable to work as the property manager, Mr. Rusk." Jolene understood Sheldon was Gordon Rusk's wealthiest client, and she was bent on ensuring Mr. Morgan's account stayed with the Firm.

"Thank you, Mrs. Anderson."

Sheldon consented to hire Jolene on the excellent word of Gordon Rusk.

"She's the woman who offered me a pair of socks the day I was in a deep depression over the passing of Blossom—Hire her."

"Are you sure?"

"Yes, In the meantime, please search for a competent property manager."

"Done," Gordon said.

Jolene Anderson, the interim manager, had been on the job for more than a month; Sheldon had come in from Montego Bay on business and stayed an extra week at the Chalet. Gordon stayed for two days of golfing with Sheldon.

"How is the weather up there, Boss?" asked Dixon in a call from Montego Bay.

"Cool, Dixon. The only thing that is missing at this moment is beer—hang in there, man. I'll be back the day after tomorrow."

Mid-afternoon Sunday, Sheldon emerged from his suite and went to the lobby for a pre-planned meeting with Jolene Anderson and her staff. First, Jolene described staff job categories to Sheldon as she made introductions. Then, Jolene explained the subtleties that make the operation successful during questions and answers. Sheldon was pleased with what he had heard and turned to leave.

"Pardon me, Mr. Morgan," Jolene cut in, "Mr. Rusk requested to speak with you." Sheldon nodded and retreated for a relaxing time-out for the afternoon.

After breakfast the following day, Sheldon sat on the lattice verandah, looking out to the golf course with a lined writing pad and pen. Jolene had noticed him in that posture before, and she believed he was an author; however, when she inquired of Gordon Rusk, he informed her Sheldon had a habit of writing love letters to his deceased wife. Jolene's mind turned over in a multitude of thoughts. First, it seemed strange for a man like Sheldon to write love letters to a deceased wife.

That day, Sheldon dressed casually in washed-out jeans, a light blue long-sleeve cotton shirt, and running shoes; he was handsome, to boot. He had a habit of smiling as he wrote, and his silhouette showed very well in the sunlight. Jolene imagined him an excellent lover, one who would bruise her with the muscles that bulged his shirt sleeves.

This fabulous man was devoted to his wife long past her death. And he was the well-dressed man she had met in a park and had given a pair of socks to warm his toes on that fantastic day; here he was, before her eyes.

Her desire to free her mind from the annoying memories of her ex-husband, Tyrone and the controlling fangs of Jose Montoy was gnawing. She sighed. Would she ever experience the love a man like Sheldon Morgan could give?

Jolene could not hold back her feelings any longer; she picked up her camera, tip-toed onto the verandah, and clicked three times in a row. The first click startled Sheldon; he did not see it coming; the second click caught him wide-eyed in horror, and he showed a polite smile on the third click. Sheldon furrowed his brow. The moment left him stunned. He did not know what to make of it.

He recognized her boldness as how city people conducted themselves—friendly; nevertheless, he would dismiss her audacious behavior as a breath of fresh air, although he would not put up with another such infringement on his space.

It had been a busy day at the shop; Mauve Moore had just sat down to rest her legs when her phone rang; her daughter Jolene was calling.

"Hello, Jojo," Mauve said in her usually melodic voice.

"Mom, I am in love," Jolene said, sounding like she was about to break out into a song.

"Jo, honey, you already told me you were sharing your bed with that polygamist lawyer at your office, and I told you it was a bad idea—a bad idea, I say."

"Not him, Mom,"…Jolene trailed off.

"Then who, honey?"

"Sheldon Morgan!"

"Sheldon Morgan—the Jamaican millionaire businessman you're working for? Baby, don't jeopardize your fantastic job—I don't like that idea."

"He doesn't know I am in love with him, Mom."

"So, how do you plan to make this work, honey?"

"I don't know yet, Mom; things like these work themselves out."

"Be careful, Jojo."

"Thank you, Mom. Goodbye."

Mauve was perplexed; she sighed deeply.

It was no surprise to Mauve Moore that Jolene called her for advice. Jolene entrusted her mother with her innermost feelings even if she had already decided how she planned to proceed. Mauve knew she could not change her daughter's mind once made up. Therefore, Mauve would not tell her daughter, I *told you so*, though she had been tempted several times.

Nightfall appeared. Rain clouds were ready to sprinkle showers. Sheldon turned into his private Suite at the far end of the Chalet on the fourth floor. He leaned back in his oversize chair, reflecting on the day's events. He was puzzled that Jolene Anderson photographed him seated on the veranda earlier in the day.

Completely taken aback, he pulled Jolene's dossier out of his desk drawer and noted her temporary status from Gordon Rusk Law firm would end when Gordon found a suitable property manager to replace her. Then, he would find out the reason for Jolene's show of unusual interest at an appropriate time. In the meantime, he waited for the chamomile tea he had requested from the dining room to be delivered.

It was seven-thirty at night; Jolene pondered her behavior; she had photographed Sheldon Morgan without his permission. There was a sense she had stepped out of her league; she would write an apology letter to Sheldon and ensure it contained convincing remorse. Then suddenly, she noticed Olga, the dining room helper, walking toward the elevators carrying a covered tray.

"I will take the tray to Mr. Morgan."

"Thank you, Mrs. Anderson."

Jolene wore a red polka-dot long skirt, a white button-front cotton shirt, and a red pump. Her hair, pinned in a bun at her nape, could come loose in a moment; she entered the elevator to the fourth floor and then Sheldon's Suite.

The knock startled Sheldon. He reached for the doorknob and opened the door slightly. Jolene Anderson stood at the half-open door with a tray in her hand.

"Mr. Morgan, I brought your tea, Sir." She said and waited for him to take the tray. Sheldon was surprised to see Jolene standing at the door of his suite.

He thought for a moment; *Damn, she is playing a game with me.*

"Thank you, Mrs. Anderson." Sheldon reached for the tray; Jolene advanced around him and put the tray on top of his desk.

Sheldon paused. It's been a long time since he had to manage a situation like this; nevertheless, he would remain professional.

"Mrs. Anderson, you were out of line this afternoon; while I was relaxing on the verandah, you photographed me without my permission!"

Sheldon rested his hand on the doorknob.

"That is why I am here, Mr. Morgan—to apologize—I crossed the line, and I am here to apologize."

"An appropriate apology would be one in writing, Mrs. Anderson."

The look of remorse was visible in Jolene's eyes; she handed Sheldon the letter of apology she had pre-written.

"No worries," Sheldon said.

"Thank you, Mr. Morgan." Jolene came closer and kissed him on the mouth. For a moment, Sheldon thought of brushing off her action, but a twitch from a place that had been dormant for a long time propelled him to pull her to him and respond with an open-mouth kiss.

At that moment of tension, Sheldon was unsure about Jolene's expectations. Should he go farther, or should he immediately ask her to exit his suite? His good manners suggested he ask her to leave. But suddenly, Jolene grabbed his face between her hands and kissed him intensely.

Sheldon had been abstaining since his wife's illness and subsequent passing. He was unsure how to navigate a tense situation like the one he found himself in. Jolene had decided, given the opportunity, she would take the lead. She touched the bulge in his lap, released it from its hideaway, and brought it to a substantial rise. She held it between her fingers like a prized trophy and gently worked it as he moaned and squirmed; he wanted her sexually. He attempted to take over, but Jolene would not let him. She sat in his lap and slowly worked his hardness. Passionate groans escaped his lips in succession, and when she saw that he had arrived at satisfaction, she said, between panting, "I promise to do it again if you let me." Sheldon expressed emotions that left him breathless. She led him to the bedroom and finished the job to his satisfaction. He lay still, unsure of the correct after-play. Finally, he fell into a deep sleep.

Jolene had shown Sheldon her heart. It would not matter if he never spoke to her again on social terms; if she had to quit her job, she would go with the memory of satisfying a man who waited too long to fulfill a yearning. Moreover, she admired his faithfulness to his wife, despite her passing. She watched him asleep; his brow still damp with sweat— she could tell the moment was a long time in coming. She kissed him lightly on the lips and lay beside him.

Sheldon awoke at 3 in the morning to soft breathing next to him. He shook his head vigorously; the memory of the hours earlier was slowly returning. He reached through the darkness for the lamp switch on the night table and turned it on; he recognized Jolene in his arm. He sighed. He was unsure whether to acknowledge he and Jolene had had intercourse though it might be the case because he and she were lying undressed beside each other.

Jolene woke up.

"Good Morning Mr. Morgan," she purred. "Before I go to the office, may I say a proper *Have a wonderful day*?"

Sheldon did not refuse her request. Instead, he allowed Jolene to say *Have a wonderful day*, her way, and he savored it. After that, though, all he wanted was to be *normal* again.

Back in her suite, Jolene showered and dressed. She had time to contemplate what had transpired, how her misbehavior had gone to the highest level. Would Sheldon come back for more of what she had given him? She hoped so. She dared not tell her mother she had gone all the way with Sheldon; her mother would not like the idea.

Her mother's cautious words resounded in her ears. *Sheldon Morgan—the Jamaican millionaire businessman you're working for? Baby, don't jeopardize your impressive job— I don't like that idea.*"

CHAPTER SEVENTEEN

Sheldon had to be at Pearson airport in Toronto by eight the following morning. Mason was on-call to be at the Chalet entrance waiting. So Sheldon hopped, skipped, and jumped out the Chalet's front door; his luggage was already in the trunk of the Ferrari.

Sheldon experienced disquiet from the night before, even if the thought brought a twitch to his loins. He forced a smile.

"Good morning, Mr. Morgan; you seem well-rested, Sir."

"Good morning, Mason." Sheldon ignored Mason's *well-rested* observation.

"Mr. Morgan, I can grab coffee at the corner store before we hit the highway."

"Thanks, Mason, no coffee for me this morning."

Sheldon slid in on the soft leather front seat, buckled his seatbelt, and reclined.

Early morning traffic along the highway was light; Sheldon opened the window beside him an inch to let in the fresh morning breeze. He remained quiet. Mason knew not to strike up a conversation unless Sheldon initiated one. All Sheldon wanted was to be at the airport on time and be ready to get on board.

Airport Check-in was smooth.

He stopped at the coffee kiosk for a small caffe latte and a cream cheese bagel; he heeded the boarding call, boarded the plane, and sunk into his first-class seat. He was relieved when the captain announced the plane's altitude and the unbuckle seatbelt sign came on.

Sheldon replayed the scenes from the previous day repeatedly in his head. *"I am confused,"* he said to himself. Nothing confuses Sheldon Morgan, his reliable thinking never lets him down, but this time he screwed up. Jolene was insistent in her sexual interplay, which confused him; she carried the ball, so to speak, and in all honesty, he let her; he did not know how to stop her.

Had he been a target? He was baffled, unsure of what to make of the incident. He sensed a sticky situation; he shook his head from side to side.

His devotion to his deceased wife was not a secret; he hardly noticed other women. He was over sixty and committed to working hard. He found happiness in his businesses and the wealth he accumulated. What happened between him and Jolene was a mistake on his part. He could not put the toothpaste back in the tube. However, he would find a way to nip the situation in the bud.

He might confide in Dixon; he needed an unbiased opinion. He would not expect high-fives; Dixon would not bullshit him. However, he would be wise to think twice before he confides in Dixon on a sensitive matter, such as the one he faces. In any event, he is willing to admit his recklessness.

Sheldon reflected on his conversation with Gordon Rusk the day he approved of Jolene's employment at the Chalet.

I recommend an interim assignment to get Jolene away from the claws of Jose Montoy.

What's going on with her and Montoy?

Montoy suggests she lives with him, but she wants none of it. Montoy knows she is struggling to afford a decent place to live; after her messy divorce and a court order to support her two sons.

She couldn't afford a decent place to live after her divorce, you say.

That was what she told me.

Sheldon considered that unless he were willing to commit to Jolene, a sexual relationship would compromise his integrity.

Dixon was sporting a bright smile when he picked up Sheldon at Sangster's Airport. A drizzle had started. Sheldon turned on the car radio. "Let's hear what's going on in the world." He said.

The five o'clock news was in progress—*rival*

Company employees attacked Morgan Earthmoving and Construction Company while CEO Sheldon Morgan was out of the country.

"What the hell is happening, Dixon?"

"Everything is already taken care of, Sir."

"Everything? Like what? Take me to the office."

"You should go straight home and rest, Sir."

"Dixon, don't fucking tick me off…you heard me---turn around and take me to the office."

When Sheldon arrived at head office, curious onlookers were milling around behind yellow tape. The back door of an ambulance was open; two police officers conversed.

Sheldon leaned against the driver's side of the SUV, his hands crossed on his chest and his legs crossed at the ankle. "What happened here?" he asked in everyone's earshot.

A policeman came close to answer his question. "One man was taken to the hospital; one man was arrested," the police officer said.

"What for"

"Gunshot"

"Gunshot; why?"

'I do not know, Sir; I understand the fight ended in the parking lot with shots fired. We're mopping up now—the situation is under control."

"Dixon—You knew this was happening? This business of gun-toting guys running around on my premises makes me nervous."

"The boys were in the lunchroom, Sir; an argument started over a girl."

"Then what?"

"The next thing I know, a brawl broke out in the parking lot. Someone fired shots to break up the melee. Somebody got hurt."

"What the hell, Dixon—this is not the wild west."

Two of Sheldon's colleagues walked into the conversation, and one of them said, "The police have everything under control, Sheldon."

"Sorry, Sir, I wish you hadn't known about this until tomorrow after you have rested." Dixon cut in. Sheldon was exhausted.

Dixon drove Sheldon to *Blosseque*. It was already midnight.

"Boss, I am too tired to drive myself home. May I have a rest here tonight?"

Sheldon pointed Dixon to the guest rooms. Dixon stayed awake, on guard.

Sheldon never slept that night. Instead, he walked the floor, trying to absorb what had happened the previous evening at his office.

At three o'clock, the alarm went off.

Sheldon shuffled into the kitchen. First, he made his usual bacon, eggs, toast, and coffee; then, he juiced oranges and poured two tumblers full.

Dixon came into the kitchen. "Morning, Boss; I heard you walking the floor last night."

"You didn't sleep either?"

"No, Sir, I wanted to be awake, in case…." he trailed off."

"I sleep less at night—come, let's have breakfast."

Dixon ate breakfast with Sheldon, brought him up to date on on-site activities, and then left for work. Unfortunately, Sheldon had forgotten to tell Dixon about his wild night with Jolene at the Chalet.

CHAPTER EIGHTEEN

Chalet in Collinwood

The phone call Jolene Anderson received from Jose Montoy came as a surprise. In a heated conversation earlier, Montoy had insisted Jolene not back out on her commitment to being his mistress. However, after a lengthy argument, he agreed not to contact her again.

Jose Montoy was brash when he called. "You are due to have lunch with me the day after tomorrow; don't pull out of it, or else…."

"Or else….?" Jolene countered.

"I will let the cat out of the bag that you are still sleeping with me."

"Bastard"

If not for her scheduled appointment in California, Jolene might have accepted Montoy's request to have lunch.

"I have a lot of stuff on my plate; I fly to California on a business trip day after tomorrow morning."

"Sorry, Jolene. I didn't mean to trouble you."

"Not at all, Jose; we will do it another day." Jolene was cordial.

Jose applied well-thought-out plans, so Jolene considered there had to be a practical reason for Jose's invitation to lunch after agreeing not to see her again.

She had heard from Irene, the receptionist at the Firm, that Jose was considering leaving and starting up his own law office. Jolene would never say never; she would lunch with Jose only to hear about his plans and whether there was a place she could fit.

It was 10 p.m. in Jolene Anderson's suite at the Chalet.

"Hello, Mom—are you up?"

"I am up now—what's the matter, JoJo? Why are you calling at this hour?"

"Nothing is the matter, Mom. I am busy working—working Mom."

"Are you still at the office?"

"I'm in my suite."

"If I told you once, I've told you a thousand times, don't take office work home; it gives you insomnia."

"It is not the work that gives me insomnia, Mom; it's Sheldon—I can't stop thinking about him. I feel like phoning him this minute."

"Don't do that—you'll ruin your relationship with him."

"Mom, you're wise—thank you; goodnight."

Jolene needed a sign saying stop or go. She needed another opinion. Jolene rested her hand on the phone receiver, then pulled back from calling Sheldon. As she waited to hear her thoughts, she replayed the scene where she made torrid love to Sheldon Morgan. His moans and groans were still fresh in her mind. She wished it would happen again; she could not rest on her laurels now; there was more work to get Sheldon stirred up even when he was away from her. Moreover, Sheldon's phone calls from Montego Bay to the Chalet were purely business; it seemed he was never available to speak with her on simple terms.

As the night wore on, she grew anxious, and the itch to phone Sheldon was compelling. It did not matter that Jolene's mother was not on board; Jolene would override her mother's advice.

It was minutes to four in the morning at *Blosseque*, Montego Bay. Jolene thought long and hard about waking Sheldon up. Then, finally, she lifted her phone and dialed.

"He shouldn't feel like I am desperate to hear him," Jolene said out loud; her favorite flannel PJs felt uncomfortably warm.

That morning Sheldon woke up at 3, astonished by a strange dream; and discovering a sticky mess on his boxers that made him uncomfortable.

After a cold shower, he put on a fresh pair and tossed the soiled boxer. He dressed and strolled down to the kitchen to make breakfast, still moody from the dream experience. The phone rang.

"Who the hell is calling so early in the morning—hello?"

"Good morning Mr. Morgan; I am sorry to call you at this hour—Jolene here."

"So you were the one who messed up my dream."

"I am sorry, Sir; I had no intention of messing up your dream, though I hope the experience was satisfying. Remember that I will be jetting to California on a fact-finding tour of Singleton Productions regarding the documentary deal. I hope Marvin Singleton will be on-site for any questions I might have. I will brief you as soon as I return." Jolene paused.

"Sir—pardon me—about your messy dream—how often does it occur?"

Sheldon pretended not to hear the question.

"Thank you for updating me, Mrs. Ander....Jolene, I hope there will be time for you to shop in a few high-end ladies' department stores in California—spare no expense on the company credit card."

"Thank you, Mr. Mor...Sheldon."

Jolene smiled. She was satisfied that Sheldon dreamt about her and had experienced an orgasm. However, she could not hold back now—onward with care—shouldn't do anything to make Sheldon back away. Jolene reminded herself that she did not know intimate things about Sheldon, except that he often wrote love letters to his departed wife. So she assigned herself to take care of his sexual needs.

Jolene considered her future at the Chalet and her relationship with Sheldon Morgan, the remarkable multi-millionaire she was head over heels in love with. She realized the frustration she had been feeling, which made her stressed, was fear of Sheldon's rejection. He had visited the Chalet three or four times that year, and his phone calls were strictly business. If Sheldon expected more from their relationship, he would need to spend less time in Montego Bay, or she, more time in Montego Bay. She was not sure which it would be.

Nine o'clock came; she had been in the office since eight-thirty that morning. She rested her hand on the phone handle, about to call the kitchen for her morning coffee and a scone. A knock on her partly open door alerted her; she looked towards the door.

"How did you get in here."

"Reception sent me in."

"Without giving me a heads-up. What in God's name brought you here?"

Jolene was never pleased to see her ex-husband, Tyrone Anderson. Uneasy is how she would describe it, for sure. Tyrone's unannounced visit made Jolene nervous.

"Aren't you going to invite me in?"

"No invitation to come any closer; state your

reason. Tyrone, are my sons okay?" was Jolene's concern. She stared at Tyrone with wide-open eyes.

"Our sons are fine. However, their support payment was not in the bank account yesterday."

"Damn. It's only been three days late; are you that desperate?" Tyrone had only been interested in the support payments he received from Jolene each month, and he threw a fit when the amount was even a day late.

"Our boys live well."

"Bastard! I know about your drinking habit—church-man."

"Where are my boys, anyway?"

"In the car, but they don't wish to see you."

"Fine! How long will you and your mother get away with keeping them from me?"

Jolene had kept a friendly relationship with Tyrone, hoping that such an effort would curry favor with Yvonne, her mother-in-law, for regular visits with her sons, but it had not worked out that way.

Tyrone's status was the ex-husband of Jolene and the father of her two sons, just that; they had nothing in common except their sons, and apart from that, Tyrone should have nothing more to say to Jolene other than to keep her informed of the boys' health and progress in school.

Tyrone surveyed the office with sore eyes; he touched the urn close to him.

"You got it going on in this place, Jolene."

"None of your business Tyrone—take a hike."

Tyrone turned to leave, "A friendly reminder Jolene, the travel agency requires the balance on the boys' trip to Disney World as soon as possible."

"Thanks, Tyrone, I remembered—goodbye."

"Was nice talking with you." Tyrone gave a satisfied grin, then he paused at the door and said;

"How is your love life? He was casual about it. "My love life is fine. How is yours, Tyrone?"

Tyrone was surprised. Jolene repeated the question back at him. He often wondered why Jolene had taken the job as a property manager at the Chalet complex.

She is an intelligent lawyer, a tough, fair-minded prosecutor, and an all-around nice person. Unfortunately, their marriage did not work out, but Tyrone accepted that it takes two to tango.

"I have no time for a love life; I am caring for two growing boys and involved in church, and that's enough for me."

Tyrone had started to build a church with a small congregation. He had immersed himself into his pious, religious life for the reason Jolene had not figured out; to be sure, Tyrone would not be committed to anything that could not bring wealth.

"Sounds like a good life to me," Jolene said mockingly. Jolene watched Tyrone from her office window as he drove off with her two sons. Then she made her way to the front door. A cab waited under the canopy to transport her to Pearson airport.

CHAPTER NINETEEN

Turnaround to the Chalet in Collingwood was quicker than Sheldon expected, and although he loved being there, the atmosphere felt different with Blossom, not with him. Nevertheless, he consistently enjoyed Collingwood, especially the downtown activities.

Travel to the Chalet allowed Sheldon downtime while on business. Dixon had expressed concern that Sheldon had been working at both ends—at home in Jamaica and abroad in Ontario. Still, more than anyone else, Dixon understood that for Sheldon to fully recover from his loss of Blossom, he must do things his way.

"Sure, Boss, a little golf and relaxation while you are away is good for you, though you could just as well go golfing right here," Dixon had said.

Singleton Productions Company out of

California had requested a meeting with Sheldon Morgan and his associates to discuss filming a documentary on the Millionaires segment, with the Chalet property as the backdrop. Sheldon agreed to meet Marvin Singleton, head of Singleton Productions, at the Chalet after Jolene's fact-finding meeting in California.

"Glad you agree to meet with Singleton," Gordon had said over the phone

"Please prepare individual overnight suites for the parties involved." Gordon Rusk told Jolene.

Marvin Singleton and Sheldon arrived at the Chalet directly from Pearson airport. Peggy had alerted Mason of Sheldon's flight and time of arrival.

It was a warm summer evening. Sheldon glanced up; the sky was clear, the sun seemed ready to go down, and a calm wind passed by his head; he smiled. He wore plain, long sleeves, a button-down shirt over blue jeans, and sneakers.

Mason beckoned to Sheldon from the curb outside the airport. He was standing at the passenger side of the Corvette, waiting to receive him.

"Good to see you again, Mr. Morgan. I hope you enjoyed the plane ride," Mason said pleasantly.

"I caught up on some paperwork while sitting in first class." Then, Sheldon noticed the switch in sports cars, "Where is my Ferrari, Mason?" Sheldon asked.

"At the mechanic shop for maintenance, Sir."
'What kind of maintenance, Mason?"

"Routine maintenance, Sir."

The drive from Toronto to Collingwood was peaceful. Sheldon enjoyed the calm wind that trickled through the slight opening at the top of the passenger side window.

"Sir, would you like me to turn the radio on to classical music?" Mason asked.

"No, thank you—jazz is fine."

Sheldon remembered his trips to the Chalet property in Collingwood with Blossom at his side. He recalled how fascinated he had been by the vast highway with vehicles zipping by.

Night lights had started to come on as Mason exited the highway and turned onto the road that led to the estate. The Chalet was where Sheldon and Blossom spent the months of January to March every year. Mason observed Sheldon's quiet reflection.

"You and Mrs. Morgan had fun up here," Mason said.

"Right, you are, Mason."

So Mason stayed at the Chalet for a week to tend to Sheldon's drive-around needs.

Jolene Anderson had been standing at the reception desk talking with Marvin Singleton, head of Singleton Film Productions; he had arrived minutes earlier. Her heart skipped a beat when she noticed Sheldon entering the elevators; she checked her wristwatch and saw that Sheldon had arrived earlier than scheduled—traffic on the highway coming in might have been lighter than usual.

Sheldon proceeded to his suite on the 4th floor. He kicked his sneakers off and stretched his long legs out on his recliner, grateful for a good night's rest.

Jolene directed Singleton and his party to their suites on the 2nd floor. She considered ringing Sheldon in his suite to welcome him; instead, she made tea and carried it on a tray.

Sheldon's door was ajar. Jolene knocked.

"Come in."

Jolene stood at the door, waiting for Sheldon to advance her further into his suite.

"Welcome, Mr. Morgan." Jolene had changed into an evening attire of a slinky powder blue open arm-hole jumpsuit and white sandals.

Sheldon's eyes stayed on Jolene for a moment; he beckoned her in.

Jolene stepped closer; she was cautious; she kissed him on the cheek. "Are you okay? Something wrong?" she asked, feigning concern.

"No. No. Nothing is wrong. I am not sure I'm ready for you now," Sheldon said teasingly.

The tongue-in-cheek response from Sheldon did not faze Jolene; she returned the joke, "Ready or not, here I come." Sheldon smiled. He studied Jolene for a moment; she had a beautiful smile. Jolene came a bit closer. "Let me get you ready, she said and unhooked the one clasp that held the front of her outfit. She gently put Sheldon's face against her open chest. He quivered. Her power made him forget who he was. She felt his rise against her warm body.

"Wait for me in the bedroom," Jolene ordered. She poured two glasses of Chardonnay and entered the bedroom; the front of her V-neck jumpsuit had already given way to its contents.

Jolene had enormous sexual power; Sheldon could not control himself, even as he let her lead during intercourse. Jolene understood the game she had been playing; it called for restrictions on their part. But, on the other hand, Sheldon had been sexually starved, and she was prepared to cater to his need for a woman.

Jolene enjoyed that Sheldon allowed her to make love to him. She wanted to be in charge of the situation; she knew he loved how she made love to him, and she loved that he pretended not to have invited her attention. And when it was all over, she said. "I have to return to my office, Mr. Morgan."

"I say you don't have to return to your office."

She turned around and smiled at him.

"I do; I have to prepare the Singleton Productions Agreement; Gordon has to review it, and it has to be ready for presentation at our meeting with Marvin Singleton."

Sheldon sulked, "If you must...." He kissed her greedily.

She reciprocated and exited Sheldon's suite.
It was midnight; Jolene finished preparing Singleton Productions Agreement; she reached for the telephone and called her mother.

"Hello, Mom"

"Jolene, honey, you know I love to hear your

voice, but your father is asleep, and he gets grumpy when he wakes up in the middle of the night."

"I'm not calling to wake up, daddy."

"We have the same phone number, honey—what's the matter, Jo?"

"Nothing is the matter, Mom; how are you keeping?"

"I am well. How is it possible for anyone to be so chirpy at midnight?"

"I'm in love, Mom."

"Still, the Jamaican Millionaire?"

"Yes, Mom, still. Thank you for answering my call goodnight, Mom."

Jolene turned the lock on her front door and walked into her bedroom. She intended to have four or five hours of sleep and be ready for the morning's meeting. But instead, the events of the past few hours kept turning around in her head. It was not like she expected Sheldon to suddenly express his love for her, for she realized who he was and, more importantly, who she was. But, if it turned out that he wanted more of what was missing in his life, she would not deny him, and, in the end, she would get what she was after—his ring. Sleep would prepare Jolene for a productive meeting.

CHAPTER TWENTY

The following morning, Jolene had to be in the board room at 10. But, first, she would go to her office to check for messages.

When she opened the door, the intercom machine on her desk had been ringing.

She grabbed the phone—Hello?

"Hello, Jolene. Did you sleep well last night?"

"Hello Sheldon, I did sleep well, though I should ask you the question; did you sleep well after I fed you your nightcap?" They laughed simultaneously.

"I was on my way to the board room for our meeting."

"I wanted to have a quick chat with you privately."

"Private chats with you are what I live for, Sheldon."

"The weather is perfect in Montego Bay. Would you consider a week's vacation?"

Jolene could not believe her ears. Since her divorce from Tyrone, she has had no meaningful relationships. Although Sheldon was presumably at least ten years her senior, she imagined the joy it would be if she were his wife. She would be happy for different reasons—he was charismatic, handsome, and a delightfully submissive lover. Moreover, Sheldon was capable of giving her luxuries beyond her dreams. Spending alone time with him was all she wanted.

"That is exceedingly kind, Sheldon. I Would love a vacation in Montego Bay." Jolene responded.

"Good—Peggy will make the arrangements." They talked more before they hung up and joined the others in the boardroom.

The timing seemed right for Jolene. She had the feeling Sheldon's request was well thought out. She was ready to be with him in an atmosphere of complete privacy. She felt like this was an opportunity to declare the extent of her feelings. She smiled.

Jolene had an end game—a long shot but a possibility; if she is able, she might have a loving and healthy relationship with Sheldon.

Sheldon casually entered the meeting dressed in blue jeans, a subtle pink plaid button-down long-sleeved shirt with unobtrusive gold cufflinks, and sneakers. Jolene maintained the corporate look in a navy blue pantsuit and dark red pump, and Gordon dressed in his original gray suit and tie. Sheldon and Gordon were early at the table. Jolene brought a hot drink for everyone; they briefed each other.

"Gordon, please give me a quick update on renovations at *Ethica Mature Lifestyles.*"

"Aluminum siding at the front of the building needed replacing, freshly poured concrete to elevate the floor of the underground parking; interior painting and replacements of draperies and curtains; upgrades to kitchens and bathrooms, and new appliances already done. You might want to see the fresh look when you feel the time is right for you."

"And you will be pleased to know that none of the residents will be displaced during the renovations. On the contrary, all of them were delighted with the new conveniences and the appearance of the place." Jolene cut in.

"You were wise in promoting Moira Morales to Director; she did a fantastic job keeping the residents worry-free through it all," Gordon continued.

"And the name change to *Blosseque for Easy Living*?" Sheldon asked.

"The name change from Ethica Mature Lifestyles to *Blosseque for Easy Living*, approved."

"This is good news."

Marvin Singleton considers himself a mover and shaker of things related to the black entertainment industry. He began his career as a stand-up comic at Kozy Korner, a small nightclub in Louisiana. But, Marvin struggled with personal charm; his jokes were full of lackluster punchlines, and bookings were exceedingly rare. Finally, he discovered his singing voice and incorporated it into his comedy routine.

Then, his career took off. Twenty years later, after scratching and clawing, he found a perfect niche in filming and producing various short documentary films about wealthy people of African lineage. The Chalet in Collingwood, with the golf course and ski hill, would be the backdrop for his next documentary, with Sheldon making a cameo appearance.

Gordon and Sheldon sat side by side around the boardroom table; Jolene Anderson sat opposite Gordon Rusk, and Marvin Singleton's colleague sat beside Jolene.

The boardroom door swished, and Singleton entered.

"My apologies, everyone—I had to make an emergency call to my director on set in Seattle."

Sheldon pointed Singleton to the empty seat at the top of the table and began the introduction.

"To my right is Attorney Gordon Rusk, administrator of the legal aspects of my Corporation and businesses; opposite Gordon is Attorney Jolene Anderson; she's in charge of operations here at the Chalet, and I, of course, have the final say in the decisions made around this table." So Sheldon said when it appeared like everyone settled around the boardroom table.

Singleton introduced his colleague, producer Mary Dyke, and took the group through a ten-minute presentation about his film production company; he restated his role as executive producer of the filmmaking component of the business. Then, he explained that the episode to be filmed at the Chalet would include the golf course and ski hill scenes. Lastly, Singleton repeated Sheldon's role.

"Mr. Morgan, your appearance in the film is around ninety seconds, as you requested."

"Thank you,"

"It will be two, might be three, non-speaking casual appearances."

"We're adding this as a final piece to the documentary—with all being okay; film production should complete in six months, then, afterward, post-production."

"And, after that, we will arrange a private viewing for you, Mr. Morgan," Marvin Singleton's production manager cut in.

"I am certainly looking forward to that. Hopefully, our private showing will be at our end." Sheldon said. "We can make that happen," Singleton said.

Sheldon listened to everyone's input and squiggled on his scratchpad. Finally, after an hour, Sheldon said, "Okay, I heard enough. Mrs. Anderson, please do follow-ups. Gordon, please take care of the possibilities; let us make it happen." Sheldon considered such a venture promotion for the Chalet.

"Shall we meet in the dining room for late lunch?" Jolene's eyes went from person to person. "Let us do that," Gordon said, looking at his wristwatch.

Lunch took an hour, and after that, Gordon said, "I apologize for leaving now; I've got to hit the highway and be in my office in time for a client appointment."

"Have a safe journey back to California, Marvin," Sheldon said with a wave.

Sheldon decided to return to his Suite at the Emerald Towers. He slid into the passenger side of Gordon's Mercedes Benz.

"Are you sure you want to come with me?"

"Yes, I'd stay for one more day of golf, but the Ivanovs invited me for dinner."

They were halfway into their journey on the highway. Gordon had been reminiscing about when he first started his law practice and how he had intended to practice a combination of corporate, employment, and real estate law.

"Man—I was hesitant to work for David Clark then. Mind you; I had been doing some work in corporate law, but not to the extent that David Clark desired. But, I have to say, David Clark was a decent man; he stuck with me, and when my corporate and real estate work exploded in a big way during Ontario's real estate boom, he was with me all the way."

Gordon looked sideways at Sheldon to ensure he had been paying attention to the conversation. Sheldon nodded. Gordon continued. "Thirty years and three adult children later, my wife Eva divorced me and went back to live in Alaska. She works at a gas drilling company as a customer service person. My daughter

Jen is in law school; there is a spot for her in my firm when she graduates. All is well." Both men laughed.

Gordon Rusk would not say he had reached the pinnacle of his law practice. His firm was among the largest in the city, busy with experienced lawyers in different competencies, even though he is exclusively devoted to legal work in Sheldon Morgan's businesses and corporations in Ontario.

Gordon exited from the highway. Then, suddenly, he switched the conversation.

"When I hired Jose Montoy, he alluded he would bring along a kick-ass female prosecutor turned criminal defense attorney. I did not rail against it—the idea suited my purpose; I knew enough about the woman Montoy was proposing to bring on; I had observed her in the courtroom, and I knew about her divorce; of course, that person was Jolene Anderson."

"You didn't tell me as much back then."

"I was immediately attracted to Jolene; however, she was already living in a crazy commune situation with Montoy at his residence even though she wanted to get away. So it was helpful when you endorsed Jolene's interim employment at the Chalet in Collingwood. It seemed like a convenient way to pursue her, but she never gave me the time of day, as they say, and I never knew why. It was unclear whether she had still been seeing Montoy or abstaining after her divorce."

I'll be darned, Sheldon said to himself.

"That was a skillful deception—I went along with

temporarily hiring Jolene at the Chalet to free her from the claws of Montoy, as you suggested. It seemed like you had your eyes on her."

"It was not my intention to deceive you, Sheldon. I am telling you about this because a week ago, Jolene called me. She said she would like to return to the Firm to practice criminal defense law. I was taken aback, for I knew she loved her work at the Chalet. Around the same time, Montoy told me he would move into his own law office. He didn't say it—but my sixth sense tells me Jolene might be part of his new venture. I never thought he entirely relinquished her; she would go with him if he made her a reasonable offer. Criminal law is her first love."

"Don't be caught off guard by a resignation from Jolene."

"Oh No, Sheldon, I will have the Hiring Agency find a wife and husband team to manage the Chalet and Convention Centre."

The information Sheldon received from Gordon was unsettling. He was ready to form an opinion and not a positive one.

"Holy shit! Jolene Anderson has been fucking Gordon Rusk and Jose Montoy; at the same time, she was fucking me—that's a wide variety!" Sheldon said to himself.

Finally, they turned into the Emerald Towers driveway; "Good night, old boy; you will have a lot to think about tonight," Sheldon said and waved.

"Travel safely tomorrow," Gordon responded.

Sheldon caught an elevator to Suite 2108. He

went to sleep, and when he awoke the following morning, he thought he had had a bad dream.

"Mr. Morgan, I have to get you to the airport at 10," Mason said over the intercom.

Sheldon was relieved to be on a plane bound for Montego Bay. The words of Gordon Rusk kept rolling over in his head.

"I was immediately attracted to Jolene; however, she was already living in a crazy commune situation with Montoy at his residence even though she wanted to get away. So it was useful when you endorsed Jolene's interim employment at the Chalet in Collingwood. It seemed like a convenient way to pursue her, but she never gave me the time of day, as they say, and I never knew why. It was unclear whether she had still been seeing Montoy or abstaining after her divorce."

Gordon Rusk had been loyal to Sheldon; he had counted on Gordon since Blossom introduced them. He depended on Gordon for reliable information. But, more than anything, Gordon had been devoted to Blossom, which meant much to Sheldon. Gordon would never stand by and see harm come to Sheldon. He would never betray Sheldon's trust. It was possible; Gordon wanted Sheldon to have the information. And if there were more to know, Gordon would tell him. But why now. Sheldon pondered for a long minute. Whatever Jolene's intention, Sheldon believes she is committed to it.

And, even as Sheldon landed at Sangster's airport, he was still troubled; pent-up feelings were gnawing at him. He wanted to throw a tantrum to release his anger.

How could a relationship that seemed so right turn out to be so wrong? Sheldon said aloud.

Suddenly he blushed. How could he not, when he remembered Jolene's torrid lovemaking; he had invited Jolene to Montego Bay for more of the same, and, of course, she would serve him.

Sheldon grabbed his luggage and proceeded to the airport pickup curb. He expected to see Dixon waiting for him.

"I am here, Mr. Morgan; sorry to have kept you waiting." Peggy was waving her hand frantically from across the road.

"Not at all, Peggy; where is Dixon." Sheldon waves back.

"Caught up in traffic coming down from the West Hill Site, Sir."

"Well, thank you for coming to pick me up, Peggy."

Suddenly, the familiar car horn of the SUV sounded in Sheldon's ears.

Dixon was bright and happy when Sheldon set eyes on him. He opened the passenger's side of the SUV—smiling from ear to ear.

"What the hell are you smiling about?"

"Just happy to see you, Boss."

"That's it?"

"Yes, I had a fender bender coming in from Ocho Rios yesterday."

"So what's funny about a fender bender?"

"Peggy examined the side on which the fender bender occurred and said *Mr. Morgan will never trust you to drive him around anymore,* and I said *You wanna bet?"*

"Damn right, Dixon, I won't let anyone, but you drive me around." The two men laughed. Sheldon eased onto the passenger seat, and away they went.

PART FOUR

ALL OR NOTHING

"Your wife has been dead for three years now, Sheldon—get over it."

Sheldon inhaled and let out a sigh. *Jolene picked a fine time to start talking about Blossom,* He said to himself. Annoyed, Sheldon grabbed his truck keys from the table with a scowl and walked through the door. Jolene watched him go, tears running down her cheeks as he drove away.

CHAPTER-TWENTY-ONE

"Wake up, Mom; today is a wonderful day!" So said Jolene Anderson to her mother at 6 in the morning, the day of her departure to Montego Bay. Delightful anticipation kept her from sleeping the night before, and, in any event, she had to be at the airport three hours before her flight.

Mauve had risen at the first ring of the phone.

"Good morning, Jojo; I haven't even looked outside yet. Why is today a wonderful day?"

"I am leaving on a plane at ten this morning—Montego Bay bound."

"Jojo, you are going away on holiday. I am so happy for you; enjoy your holiday and come back safe."

"Thank you, Mom; I'll be back in two weeks."

Mauve Moore was not entirely on board when her daughter confided her Boss had gifted her the holiday. On the one hand, Mauve wanted to believe the

Millionaire was ready to solidify his relationship with her daughter; on the other hand, she was hesitant to give the relationship her full blessing.

Mauve went and sat by the window, thinking about Jolene. She had heard enough about wealthy Sheldon Morgan to know her daughter would be a lucky woman to marry him. But Mauve was worried that Jolene was behaving more worldly than was necessary. Mauve knew Jolene never told the whole story about what was going on with her. She held back details, which could make things more straightforward. Nevertheless, Mauve was certain Jolene had a motive for pursuing her liaison with Sheldon Morgan, which made her uneasy.

Snow was on the ground that morning; the highway was messy, and traffic was slow, but Jolene reached the airport on time, checked in, and all went well.

Jolene settled in her business class seat, lay back, and calmed down. Her senses were coming back, and so were her misgivings. She had agreed to holiday with Sheldon because she imagined a path to a solid relationship. Of course, it might be easy to love someone wealthy like Sheldon; nevertheless, that may be just an imagination.

Montego was balmy.so Jolene wore an outfit she thought Sheldon would admire—a floral, full-length swing skirt and a white deep vee neck top with cap sleeves. She stuffed her trench coat into her travel bag and donned her white wedge heel sandals as soon as she landed. Then, she let her hair hang loose, leaving it to the way of the winds. Jolene Anderson was pleased. At last, she is free to roam with Sheldon.

Jolene walked out to passenger pick-up; she was surprised to see Dixon had come to pick her up instead of Sheldon, and though there might be good reasons for that, she considered it a false start to her holiday.

"Good afternoon, Miss Jolene," said Dixon with a wide smile. He collected her luggage and placed them in the SUV. Dixon made sure she was comfortably settled in the passenger side. "Mr. Morgan had to be on-site at West Hill, and he asked me to come for you."

"Thank you, Dixon—where do we go now?"

"I'll take you there, Miss Jolene." Dixon did not say much during the drive, and Jolene did not ask too many questions. She knew she could trust Dixon to take her where Sheldon wanted her to be. She relaxed.

The beautifully decorated guest house, set on a mound surrounded by green grass and trees, situated outside of Montego Bay, with two helpers to cater to Jolene, was where she would stay for two weeks, and she was happy about that; she showered and went to sleep. Jolene expected Sheldon would come to her that night; she tossed and turned into a strange bed. Being alone on her first night in Montego Bay was not what she expected.

The following day, around breakfast time, Mavis, the helper, came in with a warm mint flavor drink and pulled the blinds. Suddenly Sheldon appeared. Mavis turned and exited the room.

Sheldon made a funny face.

"Good morning, Jolene, Welcome" He had a bright smile.

"I couldn't get you from the airport, myself; dangerous weather kept me back—and before I knew it, I was running late. So how was your flight?" Sheldon concluded. Jolene planted a kiss on his face.

"The flight was fine." She said.

She pulled Sheldon onto the bed; she expected him to yield to her, but he resisted; she must curb her raging emotion; she would try not to seduce him; otherwise, her holiday could start on the wrong foot.

"You are tired, aren't you?" She said.

"It's the rainy weather; it gets to me every time, and I have to be at the West Hill site early in the morning" Sheldon kissed Jolene on the tip of her nose. Jolene rests her head against Sheldon's chest.

"I hope Mavis is making sure you have everything you need," he said with a smile. "I'll call you tomorrow," he continued, then kissed her and left. Jolene was floored.

During his slow drive back to *Blossseque*, Sheldon considered how Jolene's two weeks in Montego Bay would conclude without him feeling guilty for not showing up regularly.

Sheldon took pride in being truthful; he despised untruths for as long as he had known himself. But now, he had to admit he had not been honest with Jolene. There was no question; he had lied to himself and misled Jolene in his response about the weather. So he determined things would not be the same as before, and he should let Jolene know.

Four days had passed since Jolene arrived in Montego Bay; the weather was awful and depressing. It was either thunderstorms or erratic heat. In addition, Sheldon had been busy with things he needed to do on his construction sites. As a result, he could not speak with Jolene over the phone, and Sheldon's assistant Peggy was the gatekeeper of his accessibility and time.

Jolene telephoned her grandmother in Kingston. "Hello, Grandma—I've been in Montego Bay for almost two weeks."

"You're coming to see your grandma," her grandmother shouted over annoying phone static.

"Don't hold me to it, grandma—the weather has been terrible here."

"Why you stay in Mo Bay?" her grandmother asked in her sweet rhythmical voice.

"Vacationing grandma, vacationing," Jolene repeated.

"Can't hear you, grandchild; the phone soon cut out—have to charge it up and call you back."

The telephone went dead.

Jolene sighed. It was lunchtime. She would

order beef on rye with steamed vegetables on the side and juiced carrots. She ate lunch on the Patio, and all the while, she was thinking about Sheldon; she spent many hours trying to figure out why Sheldon did not return her calls for almost two weeks.

Was he seeing someone else? Had he had enough of her? Was their secret rendezvous at the Chalet in Collingwood timeout from his work in Montego Bay? Did he even have an ounce of commitment to their relationship? "His wife has been dead for three years—what the hell was his problem?" she said aloud.

On day twelve of her holiday, the weather was awful, same as on day eleven and the days preceding; Sheldon had been AWOL all that time.

Jolene was sitting in the dining room near the bay window. The server approached.

"Something to drink, Madam?"
Jolene gestured no; then, she recognized a GMC truck coming along the driveway. It turned the bend and parked. Sheldon hopped out.

Perhaps now was when she should gather courage and ask for answers to the swirling questions in her head, but instead, she ran to greet him.

"Hello, sweetheart." Sheldon was exhausted.

Dressed in khakis, muddy work boots, and a hard hat on his head, he appeared not to have slept in twenty-four hours. Of course, she kissed him right there, but his weariness showed.

"Good morning, Jolene," Sheldon said in a

muffled voice. "Have you been okay?" He inquired.

"I stayed awake every night, hoping you would come."

"Excavations halted, heavy rains, the ground is soggy, the holes are full of rainwater, everything is a mess" He wiped his brow with the back of his hand and pulled up a chair. "I've never seen so much rain in April."

The waiter poured coffee; Sheldon sat pensively at the table; Jolene reached for a glass of orange juice and sat with Sheldon; she decided against interrupting his mood.

Finally, he said between sips of coffee, "Jolene, I can't stay longer—I've got to get back on site. I made arrangements for Dixon to take you to the airport day after tomorrow."

"You did what? No way. This is not the vacation I expected, Sheldon."

Sheldon turned and looked at Jolene, inquiringly, "What did you expect?" he sounded concerned.

"I expected us to be together—night and day—you and me. I expected a solid promise of love. You owe me an explanation, Sheldon."

"An explanation?"

"Yes. Why did you bring me down here?"

Sheldon hesitated.

Jolene continued, "to throw my heart on the floor? You never intended to commit to our relationship…did you?"

Jolene sighed deeply. She was on a roll, and she could not hold back.

"I love you, Sheldon. I thought you loved me too."

"I'm sorry, Jolene, I'm never meant to take your love for granted."

"Your wife has been dead for three years now, Sheldon—get over it."

Sheldon inhaled and let out a sigh. *Jolene picked a fine time to start talking about Blossom,* He said to himself. Sheldon was annoyed; he grabbed his truck keys from the tabletop with a scowl and walked through the door. Jolene watched him go, tears running down her cheeks as he drove away.

The following morning, Jolene awoke to a soft kiss on her cheek. "Good morning."

Jolene yawned and stretched. "How did you get in here?"

"I came in through the front door," Sheldon answered teasingly.

"Get into bed, you naughty person."

"Not now, my dear; we're spending the day on the beach; I want to look at you in that stunning bathing suit you bought in California."

"Breakfast is ready in the dining room."

"Great, we'll have breakfast and then go."

The rain had ceased, and the sun was peeping out from heavy clouds. After breakfast, on a lazy Sunday with Sheldon, the beach should be heavenly.

There, on the beach, Jolene stood before

Sheldon, looking for his admiration, wanting to move closer to him, and make love to him; instead, he was indifferent, looking back at her with a thin smile. He desired to kiss her, but he held back his emotions. Jolene turned her eyes down, hesitant to interrupt his mood, and she walked out into the sea for a swim. Then a short while later, she returned to where Sheldon had been standing.

"I had no idea you were such an excellent swimmer," Sheldon said.

Jolene searched his face, looking for a clue. "I used to be an excellent swimmer—not anymore. Let's see how you swim," Jolene said.

The body Sheldon showed was all Jolene wanted to admire.

Later, they had lunch at the local seafood restaurant. The menu was snapper fish, the day's catch, with white rice mixed with red kidney beans. Then they strolled along the shopping strip. Jolene entered an exquisite jewelry shop. They looked around.

"See something you like?" Sheldon asked.
Sheldon had noticed her interest in a diamond-studded tennis bracelet.

"You like that one—yes?"

"Yes."

"It is yours."

Sheldon and Jolene reached the guesthouse when the sun was setting. Dixon sat in the SUV, parked in the driveway.

"What's up, Dixon?"

"May I talk with you privately, Boss?"

Jolene continued into the guest house; Sheldon and Dixon leaned against the SUV in conversation.

Afterward, Sheldon walked up to the front door; Jolene waited.

"Sorry, Jolene, I have an emergency. I've got to go. Dixon will take you to the airport tomorrow morning."

Jolene was stunned. Dixon brilliantly executed Sheldon's planned exit.

Jolene landed at Pearson during inclement weather; the limousine that drove her to Collingwood pushed through heavy downpours to the canopy at the Chalet. Jolene placed her luggage in reception and scrambled to her suite. She felt ill; she felt a chill and turned up the heat in her suite. Still, she was glad to be back at the Chalet. Her vacation, such it was, was a disaster.

Sheldon had stayed away from her except for the final two days of her holiday. Was he avoiding her? Had she misspoken? Was it all about work? Why?

His actions baffled her.

He was a shy man; still, he was clever and deliberate. Jolene would not rest until she had a decisive talk with him; she would be straight with Sheldon about her holiday assessment. Jolene was ready to come to terms with her relationship with Sheldon.

Her law practice became a primary factor; she might return to law practice at Gordon Rusk's law firm sooner than she had planned.

Her mother's cautious words resounded in her ears. *Sheldon Morgan—the Jamaican millionaire businessman you're working for? Baby, don't jeopardize your impressive job—I don't like that idea."*

She would tell her mother about what happened in Montego Bay and accept it if her mother said *I told you so.* Her mother's wisdom had always been a mainstay, even if she did not always follow her advice.

She hugged herself tightly. She was in love with a man she could not have.

Later, Jolene spoke with Sheldon about her vacation in Montego Bay and her opinion about their relationship. The conversation was matter-of-fact.

"I misread the whole affair, Sheldon; I thought you were ready to take our relationship further when you suggested the holiday."

"I thought you understood that my heart belongs to my late wife, Blossom, and into my work is where my energies go."

Jolene was not surprised by Sheldon's reply.

The words stung.

They ended the conversation amicably.

The man she is in love with is a millionaire who could have any woman he wants—she cried until no more tears were left.

She expected to return from her holiday with a ring, not a tennis bracelet, on her wrist.

PART FIVE

A LOVE HE CAN FEEL

Sheldon leaned against his truck. Once again, he found himself at a crossroads in his life. His wealth was easy for him to acknowledge, but lasting anonymity had escaped him. Yet, on the other hand, his natural need for a love he can relate to, which frees him from subjection and expectations that do not influence his decisions, is the love he craves.

CHAPTER-TWENTY-TWO

August had come in with bright sunshine and calm northeast winds.

Jamaica's independence day is celebrated all across the country with bursts of events. In addition to the one-day public celebration, most people took a week's vacation, so it seemed unreasonable to Sheldon that his project manager, Dixon, expected employees to show up at the worksites after the one-day off. As a result, Sheldon ordered all construction vehicles parked and workers to be given the weekend off with pay.

Sheldon woke up early that morning and drove to the West Hill site; he would work alongside Dixon on excavating an area close by designated for quarrying. Dixon insisted the work be put on hold until workers returned after the long Independence weekend. They drove back to *Blosseque* together in the

SUV.

"Millie and I are going to the community dance later," Dixon said as they drove along the roadway.

"I will cut away from the Independence Gala early and swing into the community dance."

"The boys would welcome you, Boss."

The Prime Minister's Independence Gala was where influence and wealth came together in one place. Sheldon had not attended an Independence gala in four years. He leaned against the handrail at the bottom of the stairs in his home, deep in thought about how he would conduct himself at the reception without Blossom at his side, and decided to let things take a natural course. Acting charming in conversations about the loss of his wife, especially at dignified events, always left him depleted.

Sheldon drove the silver Mercedes Benz to the Gala dressed in formal attire. He walked into the main hall with an air of confidence. Some in attendance turned their heads in his direction and held their breaths, anticipating a nod; all had champagne flutes in their hands. He scanned the gathering.

"Over here, Mr. Morgan."

Sheldon looked across the room and noticed the Prime Minister gesturing for him to come.

"You've met my wife," the Prime Minister said, assuming Sheldon had met her. Sheldon politely nodded.

Then, the Prime Minister guided Sheldon toward a group of dignitaries, "I am sorry for your loss of Mrs. Morgan, even though it's been a while—have a drink." Sheldon accepted a champagne flute from a server and engaged in chatter with the group.

After dinner, speeches, and more hype, the band struck a heavy beat, and attendees who could still stand steady hit the dance floor.

Mrs. Anglin, Sheldon's former high school teacher and widow of a Minister of government, found her way into Sheldon's circle. "You ought not to deprive yourself of female company, Mr. Morgan," she whispered between the heavy beats of background music.

"Maam?"

"Female company, Mr. Morgan—the female company," She repeated.

"Tsk, tsk, Mrs. Anglin. I am married to the memory of my wife— a memory that will live on in my heart. I am not interested in female company—it's too soon."

"How can any sane person be married to a memory?" Mrs. Anglin went on.

"You haven't changed since school days, Mrs. Anglin."

"You might have to go far afield to find a woman of your caliber," Mrs. Anglin continued.

Thank you, Mrs. Anglin; Sheldon was polite.

The Band struck up a waltz.

"May I have this Waltz, Mrs. Anglin?"

"If the old knees will come along," said Mrs. Anglin and slid into Sheldon's arms.

The affair was in full swing, couples were waltzing, and people were chatting; the mood was conducive to changing dance partners.

Sheldon briefly locked eyes with a woman sitting across the hall in the company of two other women. He knew her as the granddaughter of Mr. Gordon, the older man who lived in James Hill. He did his best to discourage his attention, though she was the focus of his stare.

Soon afterward, old man Gordon beckoned his granddaughter to join him. She waved goodbye to her two friends and placed herself beside her grandfather. They walked towards the main door and out to the lobby. Sheldon leaned against the door, not allowing ample room for two people to go through side by side. Old man Gordon accidentally bumped Sheldon.

"My apologies for bumping you, Mr. Morgan." "Not at all, Mr. Gordon—please give my regards to Mrs. Gordon." Old man Gordon tipped his hat. Sheldon nodded in Dorothy's direction though she never acknowledged him.

Sunday morning, eight hours after the Prime Minister's Independence Gala, Sheldon sat on his Patio with orange juice in hand. He was nursing a headache from the night before; nevertheless, his thinking was sharp. Dorothy Gordon was his focal point.

At the Gala, she wore a gorgeous spaghetti strap full-length black dress that suited her slender form; her hair bobbed at her ears. She looked away during Sheldon's conversation with her grandfather, which stuck in Sheldon's memory. He wondered if she had ever been married and had children. He has had his share of misgivings; perhaps he should erase Dorothy Gordon's image from his thinking.

The image of Dorothy Gordon on her grandfather's arm, walking out the door, stayed with him. He had watched them go until they were out of view.

CHAPTER-TWENTY-THREE

James Gordon is a wealthy sugar cane farmer. He cultivates an enormous sugar cane field just outside of Montego Bay. He lives in a large home adjacent to his plantation with his wife, Jean, and their adult granddaughter Dorothy. And though Dorothy received the best upbringing, she often lamented her mother's bad luck in marriage and feared she might meet the same destiny.

Dorothy's mother, Megan Gordon, was an up-and-coming fashion designer when she married Dorothy's father, a politician. However, her three-year marriage was rocky, and amid her husband's embezzlement scandal, she went to New York to study Fashion Design; when she returned, Dorothy refused to go with her.

"Megan loved your father, but I don't think he had done much during their short marriage to make Megan happy." Dorothy's Nana Jean told her.

So, when Paul McIntosh, a Clerk in the Magistrate's court office, broke off their engagement Dorothy was sure there was something in her DNA that would make her reach the same fate as her mother.

Dorothy Gordon is fifty-eight years old; has lived with her grandparents since age two. She is an attractive woman with bronze skin and black/gray hair cut in a bob below the ears. She has worked in the Resident Magistrate Court as a court reporter for several years, the closest she came to being the attorney her grandfather hoped she would be. Her grandmother, Jean, is hopeful Dorothy will find love and happiness in marriage. But, at Dorothy's age, men who might marry her were taken, and she was growing older by the day.

August came with fine weather. Jamacia's Independence celebrations were plentiful. Dorothy and her grandparents attended the annual Prime Minister's Independence Gala every year. However, Jean was anxious about the pain she felt in her knees, which laid her up for several weeks, so she hinted that she might not make the Gala that year.

"Take your lovely granddaughter and go to the Gala, George—who knows, there might be an eligible young man wandering around in the crowd who might request a waltz."

Dorothy blushed. All the dates she had been on since the age of twenty-five, which Nana Jean told her was the beginning of her last hurrah, were arranged by Nana Jean.

"Nana Jean, you always look for avenues where I might find eligible men—thanks for caring."

"Time is flying, Dorothy," Jean smiled at her.

"If my Nana Jean believes I have a chance at marriage, then I will not pass up a possibility—I will attend the Independence Gala with grandpa. There might still be a man waiting for me."

So Dorothy searched her closet for her best gown and tried it on to ensure it fitted perfectly.

The Independence Gala was awkward for Dorothy; it was not a place she fancied though she was proud to stand alongside her grandfather while he conversed with prominent people.

The ladies wore long gowns, and the gentlemen dressed alike in cocktail jackets, white shirts, and black ties. When dinner was over, and mingling had started, Dorothy relinquished her grandpa's arm and turned to chat with the two unaccompanied ladies at a nearby table. Their conversation was about the dapper Sheldon Morgan. One or two wives with nothing to lose, but their husbands were brave enough to approach Sheldon for a waltz.

Dorothy was relieved when her grandpa signaled it was time to leave.

On their way out, her grandpa accidentally bumped into Sheldon, who had been standing too close to the doorway. Blushing, Dorothy kept her eye down.

"Pardon me, Mr. Morgan—Mr. Morgan, I am glad you are in top form despite losing your dear wife." Sheldon nodded in acknowledgment, all the while taking in Dorothy Gordon's elegance and her quiet manner.

Sunday Morning, 10 o'clock, Dorothy heard the voices of her grandparents in the kitchen. She joined both of them at the kitchen table.

"Hello Grandpa, you're up early—after all the hobnobbing at the Independence Gala last night."

"I never sleep past 8 o'clock, dear child; if I ever do, I am dead."

"Your grandpa told me he noticed from the corners of his eyes Mr. Morgan looking directly at you."

"Grandpa, what sharp eyes you have---I never saw Mr. Morgan looking at me."

"Your grandpa's keen sight has made up for his slow hearing."

"We don't mind if Mr. Morgan looks at you."

"Nana Jean, don't bet on it."

The three of them roared with laughter at once.

Dorothy poured orange juice into a tall glass and sat on the verandah.

With every sip she took, she thought about the events at the Independence Gala, and the one person that came to mind was the man she never spoke with—Sheldon Morgan.

Sheldon's fame was well-known; Dorothy secretly admired him. But, in the years she had known him, her perception went from him being happily married to a beautiful woman to losing his beautiful wife after her long illness. So, if Sheldon noticed her at the Gala, she was unaware.

Dorothy's job at the Court's office, for twenty-five years, was recording depositions which allowed Dorothy to know everybody's legal business. For example, Sheldon Morgan's Company cases were tried in her courtroom, and she was familiar with that aspect of his life.

"Breakfast is ready," Dorothy's grandmother called out.

"Be right there, grandma."

CHAPTER-TWENTY-FOUR

"I never thought I could fall in love again." So said Dorothy, in a moment of candor; she did not intend to voice her thinking.

"You've fallen in love? You do seem preoccupied of late." Mrs. Richards from the Magistrate's office ventured. Mrs. Richards was surprised at Dorothy's openness, for she never spoke about heart matters before, yet she was delighted that Dorothy shared her thoughts.

"Yes, I am in love, and it is making me crazy."

"Sounds crazy good to me." Mrs. Richards smiled at Dorothy.

Friday afternoon, Dorothy and Mrs. Rickards went to Cool Runnings to purchase the advertised lunch special on Jerk Chicken Wings. "I'll purchase enough for grandpa, grandma, and me," Dorothy said to her best friend, Mrs. Richards, when they arrived at Cool Runnings.

"I will purchase for John and me."

Instead of joining the long line-up, Dorothy and Mrs. Richards sat at the table, looking out to the parking lot, and waited for their meal order to be ready.

Sheldon skidded his pick-up truck into a parking spot, slid out of the driver's seat, and scooted into Cool Runnings for a quick order of Jerk Chicken wings. His clothing looked like a man just coming out of a mud hole, his work boots muddy, his hard hat still on his head.

Dorothy recognized him, and she took a deep breath and held it for a long moment.

"What's the matter, Dorothy? Mrs. Richards asked, clearly concerned.

"He's coming in here."

"Who?"

"Him."

They both looked to see Sheldon as he retrieved his order at the bar counter.

"Sheldon—my friend," called a male voice across the room.

Sheldon looked to see who had called.

"Julius, great to see you, man; I got to run, though." And at that moment, Sheldon noticed Dorothy Gordon sitting at a table by the window. Sheldon stopped in his tracks; he considered walking directly over to his friend Julius to pass by Dorothy and her friend but instead, he paused at Dorothy's table.

"Good afternoon, ladies. Have you tasted the jerk chicken wings?" Sheldon asked with composure and a reasonably broad smile."

"We will; we're waiting for our orders."

"Pardon me … my name is Sheldon Morgan."
Sheldon stretched out a hand. The ladies reciprocated.

"I'm Dorothy."

"I'm Gwen."

"It is delightful to meet both of you."

And so it is. With skill and quickness, Sheldon secured a tentative date with Dorothy Gordon.

Sheldon was thoughtful during his drive back to the site at West Hill. He was unsure how he would navigate the dinner date he secured with Dorothy. He could be casual in his approach, but he'd rather be formal. Still, he is interested in a dinner date with meaning.

"Dixon, I brought you lunch."

Dixon noticed, "You are not eating, Boss."

"Not hungry, Dixon."

Then suddenly, Sheldon said, "Dixon, what can you tell me about the granddaughter of Mr. Gordon, the farmer?

"Not much, Boss—only seen her in the courtroom taking notes. So what do you want to know?"

"I'm interested to know what she does outside of taking notes in the courtroom."

"I'll find out, Sir—how did the Independence Gala go the other night?"

"That's why I want to know more about this lady, Dixon," both men smiled.

Sheldon leaned against his truck. Once again, he found himself at a crossroads in his life. His wealth was easy for him to acknowledge, but lasting anonymity had escaped him. Yet, on the other hand, his natural need for a love he can relate to, which frees him from subjection and expectations that do not influence his decisions, is the love he craves.

A magnet pulled him to a place of unknown proportions to a woman he never gave a second look, a woman he knew little about, a woman his intuition insisted he pursued.

Sheldon waited to hear back from Dixon.

CHAPTER-TWENTY-FIVE

December 16, a week before Christmas, the documentary *Snowball,* a production of Singleton Productions, with the Chalet property as the backdrop and Sheldon Morgan making a cameo appearance, is scheduled to preview at a small theatre in Toronto.

Marvin Singleton, the executive director, actors, and others who worked to produce the documentary, arrived in Toronto from California. The cast and crew that came with Singleton were ten in total.

Mason greeted Sheldon at pick-up outside Pearson airport. He was driving the SUV Sheldon requested he lease for his travel in Ontario during the winter months.

"Mr. Morgan, welcome back." Sheldon acknowledged with a friendly smile. He slid into the passenger seat and buckled up. "This feels comfortable, Mason."

"It is as you requested, Sir."

"I am staying at the Hilton in Toronto."

"Very well, Sir."

"I understand winter weather started in Collingwood. There's snow on the ground up there," Sheldon said.

"The ski season starts early, Sir."

"I will offer Singleton Productions the ski hill for frolicking after the Preview of *Snowball*."

"You are booked-in at the Hilton, too, Mason, in the event I need to move around while I am here."

"Very Well, Sir."

The following day, while at the Hilton, Sheldon met with his investment advisor Joseph Russell and his attorney and legal advisor, Gordon Rusk. They discussed two coffee franchises Sheldon planned to acquire within the Metro Toronto area. Then, he conversed with Gordon about getting Morgan Earthmoving & Construction Company listed on the Jamaica stock market.

"I will see the stock market listing standards and then make the necessary application. These moves fit into your expansion style," Gordon remarked.

"And Gordon, I am sorry to hear Towers One and Three, Emerald Towers, have gone into temporary receivership. Can we recover the buildings, if only for Blossom's sake? She would be disappointed that David's two daughters had been experiencing financial hardship, which caused that to happen."

"I will explore ways the buildings will go back

into the hands of Dana and Camile Clark," Gordon assured Sheldon.

Sheldon also met with an architect to make significant changes to the exterior of *Blosseque for Easy Living*. As it turned out, Hilton was accessible to his scheduled meetings.

Singleton Productions had organized the preview of *Snowball* at a small theatre near the Hilton. Marvin Singleton and his crew of ten were in attendance, Gordon Rusk, Jolene Anderson, and her two sons, Fenton and Justin. Everyone went to Shanty's for soul food and drinks at the end of the pre-showing.

It was a proud moment for Sheldon Morgan.

Jolene Anderson comported herself well during tense moments in the presence of the president and CEO, Sheldon Morgan.

Later, when everyone went back to the Hilton and Jolene's sons Fenton and Justin were chasing each other in the hotel's spacious reception area, she sat in a big chair watching them. Suddenly Sheldon appeared, "Jolene," he exclaimed.

Jolene's heart skipped a beat. "Mr. Morgan, I am sorry I couldn't break away to say hello, and now my sons are demanding my attention."

"I see; still, I want to tell you how pleased I am with the work you've done in organizing this event; I want to thank you for that." His smile was sweet.

"Not at all, Mr. Morgan."

"Sheldon, may I have your attention for one

moment?" Marvin Singleton called out. "Excuse me, please, Mrs. Anderson, I will be right back," Sheldon said and disappeared with Marvin. Instinctively Jolene knew her relationship with Sheldon Morgan would never be the same.

Mauve Moore had always been Jolene's confidant. Jolene was aching to tell her what had transpired between her and Sheldon. Her mother would not have approved of her challenge to Sheldon. Still, Jolene would tell her mother she had confronted Sheldon while in Montego Bay and be prepared to accept her mother's *I told you so*. Jolene liked that her mother never probed though she always thought her mother knew more than she let on.
She phoned.

"Mom, My heart is troubled."

"What is the matter, Jojo?" The phrase *What is the matter, Jojo* sounded like music to Jolene's ears.

"It's Sheldon, Mom; he is not the same as before."

Jolene's mother understood what; *not being the same as before* in a relationship meant. She never wanted to be nosy; she only wanted to ease her daughter's pain with happy talk.

"Don't be sad, Jo; you are ten years the man's junior. Has it occurred that you might be wearing him down with all that love and affection you've been giving him?"

"Mom, it is not the love that I give him. While on Holiday, I asked him to commit to our relationship, and he backed away."

Mauve Moore became silent; Jolene checked if her mother was still at the other end, "Mom, are you there?"

"Yes, I am here, Jojo."

"Then say something, Mom, say something." Jolene began to cry

"I love you, Jojo," is what her mother said.

Jolene lay in her darkened bedroom, thinking about her situation. The pain in her heart needed more than an aspirin. She reflected from the beginning. She had said, consequences, be damn, and now she must face them and be brave about it. Sheldon had given her an answer when she confronted him.

She awoke the following morning with tracks of tears on her face. She showered, dressed, and went into the Chalet dining room. A mix of skiers, newlyweds, sightseers, and two or three writers were seated and enjoying breakfast. Jolene had breakfast of scrambled eggs, cheese tea biscuit, and coffee and then went to her office.

On her phone was a message with Sheldon's instructions, which came through Gordon Rusk's office about what needed to be done that day.

She stared blankly at the phone. But then, she reflected, if she phoned Sheldon, there would be much to confess that was embarrassing and job-ending. So she decided Sheldon might be busy and not want to accommodate a confession.

"I will phone Gordon and confide in him. But,

no, I will phone Jose; he will understand."

Jolene never denied Jose. He had visited her often at her Chalet suite. The Chalet was perfect for Jolene. She never was satisfied with sharing her man with two other women under the same roof, and Jose was willing to make the trip to Collingwood as often as necessary to satisfy the desires of his woman. Thus, a true confession to Sheldon Morgan and Gordon Rusk would be she had not severed sexual ties with Jose Montoy; she also had to give up the truth about her sexual contact with Sheldon to Gordon Rusk.

In a heated conversation with Jolene, Jose had said, "I will not let your affair with the millionaire man interrupt our liaison; I have accepted it as deception on your part and a fad on his part."

"You will not call it a fad when we are married, Jolene shot back."

"My, oh My," was all Jose said.

In addition, to be up-front and honest, Jolene considered telling Gordon Rusk why she was off-putting when he showed an interest in her. But, whatever Gordon thought was why Jolene avoided his attempt, the real reason was her secret liaison with Sheldon.

If Gordon Rusk had an inkling that Jolene had continued her romantic involvement with Jose, he did not let on. However, Jose alluded to Gordon in conversations Jolene would be a future law partner.

Jolene lifted the phone and dialed.

"Hello…..

CHAPTER-TWENTY-SIX

On his arrival back in Montego Bay, Sheldon Morgan was moody. Dixon noticed when he picked him up at the airport. Sheldon slid into the passenger side of the SUV and continued on a quiet drive to *Blosseque*.

The following morning Sheldon woke up before daybreak. He lay in bed, quietly reviewed his assets, and considered all were professionally managed; Gordon Rusk was in charge of implementing the Ontario end; Sheldon was pleased with his strategies. He was delighted with the preview showing of *Snowball*; he was excited about its promotional potential, and, more than anything, he hoped the mutual relationship he had formed with Marvin Singleton would be enduring.

The reorganization of his construction company was to his liking. The company had made great strides, and he had instructed Gordon Rusk to list Morgan Earthmoving and Construction Company on the Jamaica Stock Exchange. Sheldon hoped his employees would invest in the company by buying shares as soon as they become available.

His Project Manager, Michael Dixon, came into his thoughts; Dixon had been an employee of Morgan Earthmoving and Construction Company for more than two decades. As an exceptional employee, Dixon had a good head for the construction business and could be a tremendous future CEO. Sheldon loves Dixon's ways and encourages him to buy many company shares.

Then suddenly, Sheldon's thoughts turned to Jolene Anderson. There was no denying she had been an efficient interim Property Manager, but it was time she returned to her position at Gordon Rusk Law Firm. He would ask Gordon to make it a priority.

His liaison with Jolene at the Chalet rested heavily on him. He admitted the relationship ignited feelings that laid dormant, and after his last intimacy with her; he was ready to put a ring on her finger, so he had invited her for a holiday in Montego Bay. However, the information he received from Gordon Rusk just before he returned to Montego Bay was enough to rethink his decision. And although the conversation with Gordon was hurtful, it was what he needed to hear. How unwise he had been.

Sheldon showered, dressed in Khakis, descended the stairs, and walked into the kitchen.

"Good morning Mr. Sheldon," Caroline said. She entered the kitchen and started puttering around. Millie was in the vegetable patch, weeding and raking.

Sheldon had a mind to visit his West Hill site immediately after breakfast.

He hopped into his truck. He had started a little early, but it was a lovely day, and he could not resist taking a slow drive. Moreover, he needed the warmth of sunshine and the cool breeze.

His truck hummed along the roadway; the bright morning sun peeked through the edges of the visor. The wind remained quiet except for the occasional soft whistle that came through the slight opening at the top of the window; the experience was peaceful at 10 in the morning.

When he arrived at the site, he observed Dixon leaning against his SUV with a water bottle in his hand. Dixon updated Sheldon about the activities of the day between sips. Then suddenly, Dixon smiled and said, "Sir, I have information to give you about Miss Dorothy Gordon."

"You have information?" Sheldon was surprised Dixon came back with information so quickly.

"Sir, you did ask me to find out more about Miss Gordon, and I took your request seriously."

"When will I get this information, Dixon?" Sheldon asked, sensing Dixon was holding back for some unknown reason.

"As soon as tomorrow over wings and beers at

Cool Runnings, Sir."

"You kill me, Dixon." Both men laughed.

Sheldon leaned back against his truck and gazed across the hillside; he considered the life he enjoyed with Blossom and smiled. He wished she were with him; however, that was only a wish; he knew she could never be with him—not in this life. He was lonely, with no wife and children, and his reasoning for his odd flirtation with Jolene Anderson still puzzled him.

"I am ready to turn the page," he said.

"You said something, Boss?" Dixon had been standing nearby.

"I am ready to go," Sheldon said, stepping up in his truck and driving off.

The drive back to *Blosseque* was pleasant; Mr. Charlton, Sheldon's medical massage therapist, pulled into the driveway around the same time as he did.

"Glad I made it back on time, Charlton," Sheldon said.

The following day, Dixon arrived at Cool Runnings first; he sat at a table for two at the corner beside the bandstand. First, he ordered the meal; then he noticed Sheldon walking in; he called out, "Over here!"

Sexy, the proprietor strode to their table. "Gentlemen, your jerk chicken wings will be ready soon." The mood was pleasing. Sheldon was eager to hear Dixon's information.

"Tell me what you know," Sheldon smiled.

"So, here's what I found out," Dixon said, between bites, "Miss Gordon is fifty-fiveish, never married, grew up with her grandparents, still living with her grandparents, and employed at the courthouse as a court reporter. She bakes cornbread for her grandparents every weekend and cooks delicious pepper pot soups."

"*She bakes cornbread for her grandparents every weekend and cooks delicious pepper pot soups*. Sheldon repeated.

"Yes, Boss."

"That's it, Dixon? Where the hell is the vital information?"

"That's it, Boss," Dixon said, laughing wildly.

"Dixon, I want to know if she is dating anyone."

"Not dating anyone, Boss, not since a guy named Paul McIntosh jilted her fifteen years ago."

"Michael Dixon, you are as cunning as a fox. Excellent job." both men chuckled.

As Sheldon drove back home to *Blosseque*, he could not help but wonder if there was a woman to replace Blossom who would not think it necessary to compete with his memory of her. Moreover, this woman will allow him to speak openly about Blossom.

Sheldon turned the corner and into his driveway; another day of completion.

CHAPTER-TWENTY-SEVEN

Oftentimes in denying yourself pleasure you do but store the desire in the recesses of your being.
Who knows, but that which seems omitted today waits for tomorrow? Even your body knows its heritage and its rightful need and will not be deceived
And your body is the harp of your soul, And it is yours to bring forth sweet music from it or confused sounds
—Kahlil Gibran, The Prophet

The occasion was different. It was a date, Sheldon's first rendezvous with Dorothy Gordon. He was nervous. No. Dorothy was nervous. Both of them were nervous.

Margaret's Seafood Restaurant sat on the ocean's edge with a narrow walkway extending into the waters to a thatched gazebo. This beautiful restaurant, graced with swaying palm trees, and the evening sun slowly sinking into far-out blue waters, was where

Sheldon reserved to enjoy a quiet dinner with Dorothy. Once Sheldon and Dorothy were comfortably seated at their table on the Patio overlooking the ocean, the waiter presented the Menu. Sheldon chooses her meal of Coconut Pumpkin Bisque, Cesar salad, and Red Snapper prepared with coconut milk, local herbs, and callaloo. Dorothy complimented his choice of Chardonnay from the wine list. Both of them dined.

Sheldon and Blossom stayed a while; they converse and laugh over idioms. Then, Sheldon said, "What is your passion, Dorothy."

With delight, Dorothy told Sheldon about her desire to become a published author.

"As we speak, I am editing my memoir; I approached a publishing house ready to print, and I am excited."

"That is fabulous. May I read a couple of chapters?"

Dorothy blushed. "Most definitely." Sheldon found her blush attractive.

"And I plan to author teenage science fiction books—I love science fiction books."

"Writing is sophisticated; your grandparents must be proud of you."

"Grandpa has a few essays stashed between books on our bookshelves at home; writing runs in our family." They both laugh.

"I know of a man interested in having an author write his biography."

"And who would he be?"

"That man is me, Dorothy," Sheldon hesitated, "Would you do that for me?"

"I would, indeed," Dorothy answered softly.

Though Sheldon was hesitant to talk about himself, his feelings were Dorothy had already known much about his life; still, he would be willing to reveal more for the production of his biography.

"And your work in the office of the Magistrate?"

"I retire in a few years; I will give writing my full attention after retirement. Grandpa did not like it when I quit law school. But, Grandpa understood, I did what I thought was best for me at that time."

"You are a fascinating woman," Sheldon said, studying Dorothy.

The evening sun; had sunken deep into the waters until it disappeared. He looked at Dorothy under the dim blue lights. Dressed in off-white palazzo pants and a matching off-the-shoulder top, Dorothy was beautiful; her graying hair bobbed at the ears; her beautiful teeth showed through her smile; her eyes sparkling.

Sheldon did not ask Dorothy much about her private life; he had known enough not to make it seem like he was prying. He knew there was no male entanglement.

For her part, Dorothy Gordon was speechless. This man, who had everything money could buy, still enjoying vitality and in good physical shape, was looking at her from across a dining table, peering deep into her soul; she felt naked before him. Dorothy turned her eyelids down. She knew enough about Sheldon though she did not know if he had been seeing someone. He travels to Ontario frequently because he runs corporations and businesses over there, Dorothy, though. But there is a mystery about him that she could not pin down. Maybe she does not have to know everything about this extraordinary man because she loves him—she noticed his physique even when he wore muddy work boots and a hard hat. *I would let him kiss me even with mud all over him.* She said to herself.

They talked until late in the evening, and when he took her home, he hesitated at her door and kissed her lightly.

"I had a wonderful dinner, did you?" Sheldon said with a smile.

"I did; thank you for the delicious meal, Sheldon."

He would perish the thought if he had the nerve to kiss her again. His mother had taught him not to be too forward with a lady on the first, second, or even third date; his upbringing would not let him go an inch further.

The following morning, Sheldon had been extraordinarily invigorated. He had slept well the night before; he woke up with added strength and humming a catchy tune. He showered, dressed in sweats, and skipped down the stairs to the kitchen to make breakfast. Peggy called while he was making a drink from oranges.

"Good morning Mr. Morgan; I am calling to remind you about your appointment here with Lawyer Jones this afternoon at three. The hearing on the shooting incident that occurred in our office parking lot is coming up soon."

"Thank you, Peggy; I forgot Jones was representing us in court; remind Dixon to come to get me here."

"Yes, Sir"

Sheldon was about to go through the door for a long walk when the telephone rang in a long-distance tone. He looked at his wristwatch and answered.

"Good morning Gordon; you are in the office early this morning?"

"Didn't sleep. I had a late night at Catty's Bar with friends—figured I would push through today with a hungover." They chuckled.

"So, what's up, my friend," Sheldon asked.

"Thought I call and give you good news. I hired a competent husband and wife team to be the Property Managers at the Chalet starting Monday. I received the blueprints from the architect; for *Blossseque for Easy Living* in Etobicoke, the project will start in a week and be completed in nine months."

"Sounds good," Sheldon said.

"Jolene Anderson is back at the firm."

"You re-hired her; that's good?"

"That's not how it worked out."

"Tell me how."

'She had been on loan to the Chalet though she

had been working under Montoy's banner at the Firm— Montoy recently set up his law office in the Town of Vaughn, a place which is a few miles north of Toronto, she will partner with him when he leaves the Firm."

"I wish her well, Gordon."

"So do I."

The two men talked a while longer and then said goodbye.

The morning temperature suggested he took a long walk—the birds were lively, fluttering from branch to branch, yonder rooster crowed, and a dog barked. He snipped a yellow rose from the garden and smelled it as he walked along the trail.

The next day, Sheldon went to the West Hill plant at seven. Gath, a dependable backhoe operator, had an emergency and could not come to work. Dixon never wanted Sheldon to be concerned that work would be disrupted because of an absent worker, but Sheldon would hear none of it; he insisted on filling in for Garth.

He was exhausted when he came home to *Blosseque*. He showered, dressed in casual attire, and went into his study to relax with his audio equipment. His eyes caught the photograph on his desk of him and Blossom on their wedding day. She was sitting at his side in her wheelchair. He loved her then as he still loves her. He was at peace, ready for the rest of his life. Could it get any better? Sweeter? He picked up the phone and dialed.

"Gordon, my attorney, my friend," Sheldon said, "you work too hard; you deserve a holiday; drop what you're doing and come to Montego for a week of rest. So say yes, and I'll have Peggy make all the arrangements."

"Yes, I am past due for a holiday in Montego Bay; thanks, man."

"Hello? Father Templeton? Sheldon here; I am thinking—you deserve a week of relaxation—come down to Montego Bay in a week—if you agree, I will have my assistant make the arrangements."

"I am so happy to hear from you, Sheldon; of course, I want to come to Montego Bay for a holiday—thank you."

Meanwhile, Dorothy was at home, washing and drying the dishes in her grandparents' kitchen. Then, a cherished cup slipped out of her hand and crashed on the tiled kitchen floor. Her grandmother ran to her, and Dorothy's eyes welled up in tears.

"Are you okay?" Her Nana Jean asked.

"I never want to leave you and grandpa," Dorothy said.

You'll never leave us. "You'll live in our hearts, our whole life." Her Nana Jean said.

They hugged.

It was Saturday, a balmy day in May. Sheldon and Dorothy had a light lunch at Kathleen's Brasserie, then they strolled along the avenues, shopped at the Jewelers' stores, and then went cruising the sea for two hours, laughing, talking, touching, knowing. Sheldon moored his yacht; he and Dorothy watched the setting sun; the breeze felt a tad chilly; he put an arm around Dorothy's shoulders. For the first time in many years, Sheldon found his groove.

The inside of Sheldon's yacht was classy. Blossom had designed a most elegant living/dining room, spacious state-of-the-art kitchen, and beautiful main bedroom, equipped with walk-in amenities for wheelchair accessibility. But, shockingly, Sheldon appropriately decorated the living/dining room for a planned marriage proposal.

Spontaneously, Sheldon took Dorothy in his arms, kissed her, and walked her down the stairs to the living area. He opened the double doors to the residing room, and Renick, a local entertainer, whom Sheldon hired for the occasion, began to strum *Satisfy My Soul* by Bob Marley on his guitar.

Sheldon pulled Dorothy gently to him; she shuddered and pressed in. She did not mind even though she felt his hardness against her. The scene that unfolded next was not surprising. Sheldon pulled the ring box out of his pocket and placed the stunning diamond engagement ring they had selected earlier on her ring finger. Dorothy closed her eyes. Sheldon was thrilled. He led her into the bedroom and kicked the door shut behind him, he sealed his lips onto hers, and their tongues overlapped. Suddenly blood rushed to his point of no return and aroused him. Her thighs were at the mercy of Sheldon's hardness; he pressed harder against Dorothy, bruising her. Dorothy wanted Sheldon inside of her. Sheldon felt her vibrations; he could no longer wait to please her. He touched her breasts; her nipples became taut under his touch. He had to have them. He had them. Then he slowly entered her, she was receptive, and everything they felt from that moment on was gathering toward an explosive end. "Yes," Dorothy moaned. "Oh yes," Sheldon groaned. The explosion rocked the boat; then it hushed as the moment passed.

Sheldon and Dorothy stayed beside each other, holding hands, touching, kissing, making up for lost time, and enjoying every minute.

Later Sheldon cruised leisurely through the water before dropping anchor for the night.

"I am famished, are you, my love?"

"With you beside me? No, I am not famished," Dorothy said sweetly.

They laughed in unison. "Even so, we'll go to Margaret's for dinner," Sheldon teased.

After dinner, Sheldon took Dorothy to her home; he leaned toward her and kissed her before she exited his Mercedes Benz. Wedding bells rang softly.

EPILOGUE

Thy (my) will be done this day; today is a day of completion
I give thanks for this perfect day
Miracle shall follow miracle
And wonders will never ease.
—*Florence Scovel Shinn*, The Game Of Life

Montego Bay, June 2015

He looked out of his bedroom window; the clouds had given way to the blue sky. It was a beautiful day. Sheldon caught his reflection in the windowpane and smiled. For him, it would be another day of completion.

Father Templeton and Gordon Rusk had been luxuriating at beautiful Half-Moon in Montego Bay. They had come to enjoy a vacation, and then some, at Sheldon's expense; all Sheldon had told them were they should be at the Magistrate's office on a specific day and time.

Sheldon reached for the family photo albums on the night table. He thumbed through one photograph after the other and laughed at pictures he had long forgotten. He laughed at funny ones with Blossom. Then, he paused on the ones of Blossom in pensive poses—the way she turned her head, her pursed lips, her big eyes. Those memories jolted him to simpler moments and easier times.

That 18th June at three in the afternoon was a day to remember; the sunlight had made objects glossy, and the scattered showers that had fallen between the sunlight looked like gold dust coming down.

Sheldon regarded Father Templeton's words: *My son, you are astute; you have made appropriate decisions under challenging circumstances for as long as I have known you. I know you will make the right decision when the time comes. You have my blessings.*

Sheldon Morgan realizes his devotion to Dorothy Gordon even though ties bind him to Blossom Black. Blossom gave Sheldon Morgan all that belonged to her on earth; still, she enjoys companionship in heavenly places with her son—Jason Sheldon Black.

… the son I conceived with you and delivered in secret. Perhaps there's a price I must pay for such an ill-conceived plan … for fate has chased me down, got into my face, and made me regret—the price I paid for loving you.

—CRY TOUGH

Sheldon Morgan and Dorothy Gordon stood before the Magistrate and said, "I do." Present were Grandpa and Grandma Gordon; Dixon and his wife, Millie, Caroline and Peggy; Gordon Rusk and Father Templeton.

Sheldon, dressed in an ashen long-sleeved shirt clasped at the cuff with gold cufflinks, his silver-gray suit, and tie, complimented Dorothy's square-neck, calf-length pewter color organza dress, and coral sling-back shoes. In addition, she carried a small bouquet of yellow, coral, and pink roses. Dorothy chose not to wear a headdress; instead, her graying hair hung just below her ears.

Sheldon Jason Morgan and Dorothy Alma Gordon became husband and wife.

Later that evening, at a private dinner party at the home of Michael and Millie Dixon, Sheldon felt at peace with himself; he had put the *icing on the cake*.

The dinner party slow-rolled late into the night with long over-the-top speeches and celebrations.

The following day Sheldon rose to the familiar 3 a.m. wake-up chime of his wall clock. He turned toward the warm body next to him and savored his newfound peace. Then he gently loosened her clasped arm around his waist and tiptoed down the stairs, through the kitchen, and out the glass sliding doors to the Patio. Finally, finally, freedom came to Sheldon Morgan in a perfect way.

Later, during a quiet conversation, he and Dorothy ate breakfast. The menu was Sheldon's favorite bacon, eggs, toast, black coffee, and orange juice; the phone on the Patio table sounded, and Dorothy answered.

"Hello, Grandpa; how are you today?"

Dorothy put Grandpa Gordon on the phone speaker.

"Very well, my dear, your grandma and I are on our way to the farmers' market. Can we bring you and Sheldon some carrots and turnips?" Dorothy looked at Sheldon

Sheldon bobbled his head.

The day dawned, and the sun had risen magnificently in the east. Sheldon stretched the length of his body on the lounge, as he had done several times before. He gazed at the shapes and sizes of silhouettes formed on the Patio floor. Then he spotted an injured chi chi bird balancing on a weak stem and cheered the bird for trying to steady itself.

His new wife Dorothy was by his side The long floral dress Dorothy had on complemented her graying bob haircut. The Sunlight on the Patio was warm on their faces. Sheldon smiled at memories that popped up unexpectedly. He made a note in his diary, and then he wrote a letter to Blossom—

My Darling Bloss. I am writing to you in the year 2015.
Things happened that I liked and things I hated. But in everything, I never stopped loving you.
Jolene Anderson gave me the love I craved, the body on which I lay. And, during my encounters with her, I felt I had cheated on you. Please forgive me. Gordon Rusk hired a Property Management team for the Chalet and Convention Centre in Collingwood. You will be pleased that Ethica Mature Lifestyles is part of my Estate; I renamed it Blosseque for Easy Living to always remember you.
My Darling Bloss, a beautiful lady named Dorothy Gordon, came into my life. Her kind, gentle spirit is what I want and need. She ignites energies in me that I had carefully covered and left smothering. I Marry her. Still, the memory of you is indelibly stamped on my heart.
After all this time, I love you, still.
Sheldon.

Sheldon gently put away his pen and folded the letter. He was pensive.

"Penny, for your thoughts," Dorothy said.

Sheldon turned, looked at her, and he smiled.

"This is my last letter to Blossom," Sheldon said and handed Dorothy the letter he had written.

ABOUT THE AUTHOR

For Olive Rose Steele, writing is a natural ability and a pastime she enjoys. She founded *Let's/Have/Coffee*, an informal connection that promotes and encourages inspiring conversations about life issues in spontaneous settings. She blends her faith and spirituality in comprehensible self–healing ways and draws on life experiences to inspire. Olive Rose Steele is the mother of one and grandmother of two beautiful grandchildren. She lives with her husband, Herbert, in Ontario, Canada.

ACKNOWLEDGEMENT

Thanks to Blossom Mae Black, a fictional character nevertheless, for letting me be her voice. She directed my thoughts and feelings and expanded my interpretation of the character Sheldon Jason Morgan in a way no other alter ego could. And, her shadow remained throughout AFTER ALL THIS TIME, Still.

THANK YOU

Thank you to readers; you've waited patiently for this book and have directed my focus to characters from Book One, CRY TOUGH, in the Millionaire Series. I hope I have not disappointed you in Book Two, AFTER ALL THIS TIME, Still.

The Millionaires series, set in and around Toronto, Canada, and in and around Montego Bay, Jamaica, includes scenes that will warm your hearts.

This Series is a work of fiction, although the names of some places remain for authenticity. The Emerald Towers, One, Two, and Three, are my imagination. Suite 2108, mentioned in Books One and Two, was once a suite I occupied.

I thank lawyers who have read and will read this edition; I apologize for not expanding on legal references with more depth in the mentioned areas of law. Instead, I drew on my imagination and previous experience in law settings. Please forgive any false assumptions or impressions.

The title of this edition: AFTER ALL THIS TIME, Still, turns out to be words from a love song written in the 1980s by Country Singer Bill Anderson, who is still living. I am thrilled my thoughts presented a title such as this, though I was unaware that such a song exists.

I acknowledge all of the members of my local authors' group: *Up-close and Personal with your Local Authors*; your work has not gone unnoticed; your dedication is second to none.

Last but not least, I express thanks to my husband, Herbert. He repeatedly allows me to go into hiding during my writing spells; my daughter Sharon and my granddaughters, Princess and Precious, persistently hold me accountable to writing quotas.

I hope you will return for more in Book Three of the Millionaires Series.

Olive Rose Steele
ONTARIO, Canada.

THE MILLIONAIRES SERIES

A Review by; Cheryl Antao-Xavier, Author. Publisher, In Our Words Inc

In Blossom Mae Black, Olive Rose Steele has created an unforgettable heroine who evokes comparisons to one of literary fiction's most memorable characters—Scarlett O'Hara. Beautiful and brazen 'Bloss,' as she is called by those who love her despite her flaws and poor choices, is infuriating and endearing at the same time. If you are conservative, she will shock you. If you are a hopeless romantic, she will appeal to your heart. And if you are adventurous, prone to grab at life, and ride every opportunity towards your shifting goals, well then, Bloss will get into your head and haunt you. You will want to step into her life story and make things okay. You are concerned for her. Fear for her. Want to be her and yet not want to be her. That is the strength of Steele's writing craft. Highly believable fiction. Cry Tough is a poignant story that will stay with you long after you have read through the entire novel and reread the beginning—which is a must to bring closure to your own keening emotions—and have closed the book and put it away.

PRAISE FOR THE MILLIONAIRE SERIES

AFTER ALL THIS TIME, Still
I have waited for this second novel about the main characters Sheldon and Blossom! How could Blossom die in the first chapter of this book, I asked myself. What else could there be about her and Sheldon? Well, I was in for a surprise! —Norma Nicholson, the author of WALKING MILES IN SENSIBLE SHOES, Ontario, Canada.

AFTER ALL THIS TIME, Still…will do it to you.
Love, true love, is described by one thinker as a pleasurable pain! How true. Reading through AFTER ALL THIS TIME, Still, one can't help but agree with this statement about love. The author did a masterful job in this book…Her narratives brought the characters to life…You might have been watching a movie rather than reading this work. Bravo! Riveting and difficult to put down. Olive holds her readers Spellbound. —Review by Mr. Patrick Njoku: the author of MY MOTHERS WIFE (A Trilogy). Brampton, Ontario.

CRY TOUGH (A Novel)
I finally got around to reading this book and finished it one weekend. I found it to be quite intriguing, filled with many twists and turns and unexpected paths. I could not wait to get to the end, and without giving away too much, I must say it left me thinking.
—Marcia Porter, Ontario, Canada.

CRY TOUGH (A Novel)
I started reading CRY TOUGH and couldn't put the book down; it is fantastic writing, and the author certainly knows how to engage her reader. Thanks, Olive!
—Selina Allen, Brampton, Ontario.

In the book "Cry Tough," the writer shows that people face challenges. And that we can overcome our obstacles by praying are reconnecting to our spiritual self. Thanks for the gracious and loving inspirations you have documented in this book.
Love always.—Henry Reid, Ontario, Canada.

Cry Tough

5" x 8" (12.7 x 20.32 cm)
Black & White on Cream paper
ISBN-13: 978-0981072319
Fiction / Romance / Suspense

OTHER BOOKS BY

OLIVE ROSE STEELE

AND WHEN WE PRAY (Suggestions and Prayers for Living in Spirit)

GREAT IS THY FAITHFULNESS (Insights for Seekers of Self)

THE SOLID ROCK (Other Ground is Sinking Sand)

SELF-HELP YOURSELF (Find your "kick-ass" Mentor in a Self-help Book Vol.1)

SELF-HELP YOURSELF (Find your "kick-ass" Mentor in a Self-help Book Vol.2)

WATT TOWN ROAD
(A Memoir)

Made in the USA
Middletown, DE
09 September 2023